GEORGE SAITOH

ALL

THE

DEAD

ANIMALS

a novel

Janus Creations
TOKYO
2018

*Janus Creations, 2-9-3 Shoan, Suginami-ku
Tokyo 167-0054, Japan*

or by email to:

info@januscreations.com

www.januscreations.com

To Mick from Mayo

'My meat is to do the will of him
that sent me, and to finish his work.'

—John IV. 34

ONE

It is the second clear day after the storm, lesser than the first, less blue, less bright, less arousing. I have, it seems, grown used to the fine weather again, already forgotten the terrible wind and rain. This day has a dusty tiresomeness though it is not yet noon. It appears to be waiting, expecting me to do something in my turn. It is wasting its time. That waiting, rapidly motionless, I find insolent and turn into myself. I will not be forced into an act today. I will not be augured.

The drying leaves are still green but from their echoing rustle, almost a crackle, the furling has started. Soon she—mother tree—will stop trying and abandon them all to wind and gravity in exhibitionist showers. The tired leaves appear to be panting though some of them, admittedly, might be laughing, at least sniggering. A handful is in a frenzy that cannot be interpreted satisfactorily. 'We will not be shed.' Perhaps that is their reckoning. 'We will shake ourselves free. We will do the shedding to ourselves'. But how impossible! Nothing can shed itself. Another verb needed. Or something else entirely.

It will not be the same when the last leaves have dropped. By the time new ones come along next year I will have disposed of my love of leaves. I will love something else. But how presumptuous of me. I may not be here when the next generation emerges from brown branch-nubs, a crop of ignorant strangers, no less beautiful for their newness, if I am honest about it, just harder to love for it; harder to have sympathy for. No, love. No, sympathy. Love, I mean, when I say sympathy and vice versa. Or something in between perhaps. Who knows what I mean if I do not know? But I do know really, I mean worry. Like sorry, it leaves the mouth agape, and so better written than uttered. It does not prime the lips for a smile, like love, but for a whimper instead. I do not care if I whimper or smile, it makes no difference to me. The meaning is what counts or, I should say, the feeling.

But wait. One by one clouds hover slyly into view, bluffing rain or some other, outer, change. Their feathered edges shift and seep into, dilute the blue. They do not move me except to think of flying saucers, and for a few seconds only. I love all clouds but these mere-clouds least of all. They are tiresome, make me want to stop loving clouds altogether on their account. But I know that later, when a granite-grey lilac-buffed cumulous lurches upon me around an hour before dusk I will have to stand and stare at my norse-faced god and recall my error, and say 'I am sorry', and whimper, and though he will say 'That is all behind you, son, love us again', I will not because I will not be augured. He will not understand. He will think my sadness is great because he believes my error to be small. But it is colossal. And if he knew how colossal he would be angry at my paltry sorrow. And then I would be crushed by his ignorance, the ignorance of my god who does not yet know me after all this time.

So I do not stop loving the clouds today, and defer that interview with my northern god. No, I become grateful for them instead. I make myself love them.

*　　*　　*

'Tongue-tied are we? Tongue-tied? Tongue-tied!?'
The mistress touched the cutting edge of her upper incisors with the moist tip of her tongue, pointing at the conjunction with a straight finger. The boy faced ahead, at nothing in particular, disentangling the

voices rippling from the yard through the half-open window and into his brain. What were they saying out there? Each voice announced one individual then disappeared below the surface of sound as soon as he focused on it, and was lost. It was the same with the next one. Each voice held up one, or two, distinct syllables and then lapped against the mass, breaking up into foam. Only a scream would carry longer. One of the screams soared so high he recoiled in his seat. He had been listening too intently.

'Tongue-tied but not deaf then,' she said.

He turned his head to her and slowly lifted his eyes. White below his irises showed. He smiled generously, exposing his large front teeth. Tombstones, his mother had called them even before they were fully down. He showed the mistress his tombstones. The stretched lip of his smile shifted a neighbor that had been loosened slightly yesterday. She was lovely underneath it all, worthy of a full smile. Suddenly, the voices outside seemed to soar for his liberation. But he adjusted his concentration again until only in the lulls, where the crows were, did he hear the outside. Otherwise he poured all his attention upon her, showed her his mouth, let her look at his knuckly hands. Who was this woman? What interested her in him alone and none of the hundreds outside in the yard or the millions beyond that? Why was he so special to her?

*   *   *

It seems for the entire world that today will lose to me. So much dull white and blue-spoiled furrows my all too wrinkled memory beyond folds of hidden hope. Laid before a day such as this action of any kind is absurd. Are there not wrinkles enough? And on top of that the threatening furrows? Better the wrinkles than the furrows, richer in detail though less orderly. And better the wrinkle you know than the wrinkle you don't. And better to make sure to know the wrinkle before it is buried in a furrow. And better . . . Enough! Maybe later, then, after tea, some action, when the light has swung under, casting a cloudspell of color upon me, when there is too little time left in the day to do serious wrong. But I am not promising anything. We shall have to wait and see, all of us, who will have won, if anyone, if anything, by the end of this day. Who knows what this breeze might become, or these whitish sky-smears?

Yet if I am honest, the warmth in the air wafting through the fly-screen has me suspicious, and anticipatory. Not just of the usual lingering mosquitoes but other things besides, like longings; lingering longings for instance.

*   *   *

The mistress smelled of warm bread. It was in her voice too, and in her exposed skin, soft-tanned, imparting to him impressions of sunshine and warm colors: orange, amber, ochre, and decorative metals: copper, bronze and gold; rusted iron as well. A freshly baked turnover cooling on a tarnished tray on a sun-washed afternoon, in an orange-walled kitchen. He had the picture in his mind of where she came from, of the kind she was. Next to it, or inside it somehow, was a golden and pitted chalice, encrusted with precious stones. And yet she seemed at home in that cool moss-green room with its chestnut floor, giving off its peculiar scent of needle-fine intelligence. The watery glass of the arched windows seemed to be on the verge of tears. How must it make her feel, he thought, to look out through the glass of those high windows every day, as he was doing at that very moment.

She waited and watched him as he opened his mouth, like anyone struck by the urge to speak, then touched the tip of his tongue against the longest tombstone, sliding it along and off the corner onto the edge of the shorter one, delving deeper into himself in the process. All in silence. Her face turned livid. He closed his jaw again and tried to recover the same smile as before but it was weaker now, his lips did not part. She put the book she had been holding down beside her sandwich and cup. It was sufficient to evict a puff of chalk dust that went up willingly enough until the light shaft caught, and spun once, each solitary grain made profoundly silver before it vanished. The motion of her eyes (though they never left his they were not entirely still) resembled the rutted second hand hanging behind her on the pillar between the windows. The spent battery had the power to push against, but not overcome, the clock's inertia: tick-tih, tick-tih, tick-tih. His own eyes, he imagined, were quite still.

'If I were your Mama…' she began and stalled.

I would love you dearly! 'I…your…Mama. I *am* your Mama!' She was his Mama. 'My Mama!' He would sit in her kitchen, the citrus-scented bread kitchen, stomach nauseous with love for Mama, spinning orange pools of sunlight to a future together with his free eyes, waiting for the baking to finish, hoping his love for Mama would settle in time to allow him the pleasure of the bread she would be baking for him. Even if his love for Mama, and desire for the bread intended for his pleasure alone, were initially too much all together, or even separately, he would get used to it and not reveal fret. Nothing would be wasted on him. She would not be sorry for loving him, he promised himself.

'…I would tickle your behind with a meter stick.'

If necessary, so be it. It might not tickle but she would give up, this new Mama, sooner than other Mamas. It would be acceptable to have her tickle his behind with a meter stick, with anything, tickle anything of him with anything. With it over, he could get on with loving his Mama, and her bread that she wanted to bake just for him. But what would they drink? Meter stick gave him little to go on but her creamy-smooth skin and the stiff contortions of her slender nail-trimmed fingers left no doubt they would have milk.

*   *   *

Somewhere in Africa tribes communicate, in part, by oral clicking sounds. If you want to know more precisely where I first found this to be true it was in a Namibian hole not far from Botswana's invisible border. But it goes on in other places too, I later discovered. One time, I eavesdropped on those sounds while watching small desert frogs capable of jumping long distances gracefully, crawling awkwardly across a sloping bed of pebbles; neither type of creature could see me though I had a clear view of them all. In both cases—the frogs and the humans—the possibility of understanding something held my attention until something intervened and I had to act. I will not mention how much time I wasted. But what I came to understand, I can at present only relate in this brief way, or else in a passage that I believe will take the rest of my life and when death arrives be incomplete. I do not wish to attempt the second description; a suggestion is preferable to me. And who is to say your own curiosity, if aroused, will not be better served by your own imagined understanding of what you think mine to have been?

*   *   *

At last the boy saw what he had, the previous evening, found to be missing from its usual place: a decorative pot of quince jam, a memento from a friend's visit to North Africa. He was getting on track. A careless bump would be the end of its shelf life, or corner-of-desk life. So long as the quince jam was there, there would be no careless bumping. Careful movements created grace. Between his past and what he must face in the future was her grace. Through it, was something entirely he. He was concealed within her grace. How did she know? Did she really plan it this way?

A lemon wedge of wet under each arm stained her white chiffon blouse, and spurred his thoughts to other places that may or may not have been entirely dry either, hiding beneath French scent within her grace, delivering baking notes to his imagination in oblique pulses. 'There was a struggle…' he wanted to spectacularly begin but without knowing the ending in advance, afraid he might even be starting at the end, he said nothing, just sharpened his tongue and touched his tombstones, another smile under preparation. His thoughts became scattered all over again.

*   *   *

A freak gust throws brown, balled leaves I do not expect up. They rattle a protest, run over the flat roof edge, and then down to where I can no longer see them. All that I see is green again and, through my imagination, a bit more furled and still as frost. Until the next gust, bigger but slower, shoves the first tree over and so on across the stand. One of them, a *metasequoia*, tosses mutely. Trunked to its tip, there is no bouquet of branches to worry over, to look out for, or to watch from under. Then I know the pattern: stop, start. Erratic. I am wed to it in moments. The only thing to watch for is the redwood coaching the stricken angiosperms below its shoulders to roll with grace: 'Fan out each piece of your self,' it recommends with articulate needles flexing. 'Take the wind constantly and separately, not all at once, not noisily and destructively. Above all hang limp, not rigid. Force the wind to lift you up. That counts too! Conserve energy. Like this, watch me…See! Imagine you are like me.' And with each gust a demonstration of grace before an intermittent force.

*   *   *

There had been tubers once, he had almost forgotten. Pinks or Queens, maybe Records, in Rush. Backbreaking work (Mr. Kearney had confirmed it for him with a Brian Friel story). Filling layered brown-papered sacks, smelling of the same spare soil, more when torn. That was in his head, in with the bread, that earthen smell, and with it additional colors from a layer of dry but not parched topsoil. Dryness in graduated brown, covered diagonally by a leveret. An easy shot for his father. That was somehow part of the mistress too. It was in there with her, in there with him. On track, so far. Now there they are together in Rush, potatoing, racing even, to add to their fun. Any moment the guttery laugh of the mistress. But it had not been the mistress in Rush, but his other Mama, had it not? How could he know for sure? Was there a hug, a kiss? Anything was possible if he could help it along with some words.

'I...I...I'm...sorry Miss,' said the boy.

The quick 'sorry Miss' (there had been no comma) corrected the troublesome pout-cum-quiver mouth into a steady line. He had created a new word: *sorrymiss*. Nervous pressure vented on the esses, dislodging her eyes and they fled toward the window, her body in pursuit. And what a commotion her term shoes made then in just six sure beats! Twelve demi-beats: systolic three-inch heel, then the toe's diastole. Mama Mia! From that range he loved her even more, even with her back to him. They both looked out the window, he over her shoulder like her lover, together aligned, listening to the sounds coming through the honeyglass. He suddenly realized how sleepy he was from the walk across Dublin the previous night.

'Once upon a time, long, long ago in a village far, far away...' she began to the window. Heels and toes six times, her turned back and then a fairy tale! How suddenly everything could change and had to be re-appraised. Was she looking through, or at, the window? While the mistress narrated he alternated his point of focus because he could not be sure. It was not baking bread in a sun-flooded kitchen or potatoes in Rush. But it was nearly as good. Her voice came into its own, becalming those outside who now made up the sounds of the ancient, faraway village.

*   *   *

A solid black Alsatian, its undivided apathy for everything but its owner, passes by, and the air cools by degrees. The wind appears to have stopped for good, though who can be sure? The pinpricks of rain are so small they are all surface, impenetrable to the greying light that like fine shot they deflect harmlessly left, right and center. The Alsatian marches on. Its lolling tongue, together with its teeth and gums are like a blossoming orchid on a black bough. The sky has no color left, I am quite sure of that, unless you count whitish-grey as color, or black in the dog's case. I often do not. Today I do not. Maybe when the Alsatian passes again on its return I will find some color in its coat. But for now I fall asleep.

I awake and can barely see. The sun has come out again. Who would have guessed it? Even dirt glimmers and blinds my sleep-bleared eyes. I squint at a bright new world. On every surface there is a dab of what looks to be white: purely reflected light. There is not a faint heart in sight, glancing incident sunbeams see to that. I would love to see that Alsatian now, a purplish sheen wrought from its coat. But it seems it passed this way again as I slept.

It does not take long for growing patches of late afternoon shadow to offer my eyes a resting place to open fully. And soon enough I must look up to the treetops for any remaining dazzle, the last dregs of white. By now most of the white is reduced to one or other color, revealing what it really was: overexposed to white for only a spell.

*   *   *

'…there lived a little boy who didn't like to speak. But he knew many languages. He loved each language so much that it made him suffer to speak just one of them and, in turn, to listen to the other villagers speaking, because they could only speak one language. But he was a good boy who loved his Mama and Papa, and the other people in his village. Each day he did his best to speak and listen to other people, all in the same language, and though he suffered and felt like crying he knew he was doing the right thing, and told nobody about his regret for those unspoken languages that only he knew. The boy had never been outside of his village and had no way of knowing if anybody else knew these other languages. Privately, he worried what to do about his strange problem. For until he found somebody to speak with in these other languages, he felt certain he would go on suffering. He worried there was nobody and that he would have to endure the same language, one of many, each day for the rest of his life.

'One day when he was alone the boy imagined so powerfully that somebody was with him who spoke the other languages that he knew, he believed that this person really existed. This imagined person said something in one language and the boy immediately understood and responded, not with the dread that he usually had when speaking, but with great pleasure. Amazingly, when he switched to another of the languages during the conversation, however suddenly, the imagined friend responded in that language. And together they spoke all the languages the boy knew…'

An apparition suddenly appeared on the pane. Or was it sudden at all? He could not be sure. It was her face and shoulders, and her eyes. It meant she could see him too, from there, without turning around. By facing the window, he saw how she could see inside or outside the room with just a tightening of the muscles inside her eyes. It was because of a film of dirt. During the last few moments, he now realized, she could have been observing him. There was nothing he could do about that now, except worry, and so he did. So much so that hearing the rest of the fairy tale caused him almost unbearable suffering, for now he had to assume she was watching him without being sure.

'...The boy had discovered a great pleasure on that day. Over the following years he spoke with himself through his many languages whenever he could be alone. More and more he avoided people as his private conversations became more satisfying and interesting than any he could have with real people. For the boy, this didn't upset him directly, because he felt he was doing what was right for himself—to him he was keeping something alive that, otherwise, would die. It was his duty. But he knew it upset the people who knew him and, because he loved them, it caused him to worry about their suffering. He spent so much time alone that he almost forgot how to speak in the villager's tongue. And when he was not alone, he could only listen because the effort of forcing himself to speak became too great. Only to his Mama and Papa did he still try to speak. But then what he said sounded strange to them. It were as if the words had no meaning, as if he had chosen them at random to make a sentence that was quite correct in one way but wrong in another, at least to those that heard him. But, to the boy, he was speaking as he had always done. Of course this upset his parents, which in turn made him sadder. "Why are you speaking like that?" they seemed to say with the same expression on their faces. "Like what?" was the question in his own mind. "I am just saying the things that everybody around me says. Why do I get these strange looks?" he wanted to say, but could not because they had not accused him of anything. It was all in his own mind. But he never said it. He was truly at a loss, and the harder he tried to speak well, to make them happy, the more painful their looks became. It seemed as though they thought he was mocking them. And, after some time, when he had finally given up trying to speak well, he found that he could have some fun, and that fun to some extent helped make him feel a little better when he received those painful looks. The boy found that the language of his village that he had such a dislike for consisted of a handful of expressions that he would randomly use whenever he had to speak. He began to enjoy more and more the discomfort he caused his parents. Yet this fun, which was developing into a sort of revenge against them for making him feel so terrible when he had tried to speak earnestly, was nothing compared with the joy of being alone, speaking other languages, with nobody else around, with no hurtful looks. Alone he could express through his own words every thought inside his head perfectly.

'As time passed the boy began to suspect that his Mama and Papa didn't love him. They made less demands for him to speak. He was sure they were as tired of him as he was of them. With that thought he felt that love for them had become impossible. Then, one night there was a fire while everybody slept. The boy's house was one of the first to burn. As smoke and flames consumed each room the boy woke up in time to escape and save himself. He stood outside, helplessly watching the house go up in flames. On that night the boy's parents slept deeply, and did not wake up until it was too late. Staggering through the heat and blinded by the smoke they gathered in one upstairs room near a window. Through that window, from the safety of the street, the boy stood and he saw, among the flames, a…'

Plasticware basins melted in his mind. Blistering paint turned black and then burst alight, even in this aquarial room. A shriek and crabby scratching split the sounds of crackling timber and hissing draughts that rushed through the window gaps. The boy rolled his eyes around the green walls and shellac floor, pushing his large hands together through his pressed thighs despite knowing she might be watching him. The pot of quince jam had changed sides, gone with the flames and screams, and grown active, constantly creeping into the corner of his avoiding gaze: a potential flashpoint inside this room. As if it would help, moisture gathered around his eyes and so he had to be careful about blinking. Each eye puckered for a blink. 'Stop it Miss. Finish it Miss.' He said nothing in fact, but he moved his mouth and as soon as he did he felt sure she had seen it, and his wet eyes as well. He looked at the small pits at the sides of his wrists and his eyes dried out a little in the still air. If there had been a real draught he would have blinked. But there was not and he did not. And then she ended the story.

The racket outside the window had surrendered to the end of lunch bell, and at last it was time for the boy to say farewell, and to go from the room knowing something the mistress must have suspected: that he would never see her again.

*   *   *

That is one version of how it was. It is the version that fits with today, at least fits enough to be let loose around the garden for exercise and for a voidance. To do nothing about the problem really, merely burn a little energy for its own sake, appear to be ridding. Yet it gives my heart and blood the sick quickening I can no longer do without, and cannot always have. So it has me in thrall, wondering what if I could remember yet another version. What if I could not remember any? That is how I spend my in-between moments, full of wonder. Yet I am an old man. I drink glass after glass of water, holding the rim to my lips as long as I dare, not because of my thirst but for what I see when I look inside through the medium of water and glass: silvery mirrors, coronal diffusions, distortions, duplications and reductions. It is not really like that, I say to myself, when I put the glass back down and look around me, swearing to die of thirst if necessary to make my point, to make myself believe my point. Call me what you may, a coward if you like, a hero if you understand, when I tell you that I habitually pick up the glass again, but when I least expect to, and without presuming to know what I will see, or what I will come to believe about the past for the duration of the seemingly endless future.

TWO

I do not mind the waiting at this time of day, when it is clear, as it is now. So much change over a brief interval. It hardly feels like waiting at all. From that first yellow star to the last seam of heat sinking unto the horizon—so much change. It leaves me beside myself. Just like you I find myself trying to freeze the change with my concentration. I cannot help it. It is the effect of that desire to be fully aware. I do not think either of us will ever be able to freeze the change from day to night with our concentration, will we? I am almost sure of that. But we can watch it all over again another time, can we not? Is that not almost the same thing? Now it is coming on. I am fortunate it is so clear this evening. I feel blessed. Please wait a moment. I expect I will return to my story in a while. Forgive me. I am ashamed.

*　　*　　*

Seven years before that final visit to the mistress's office the boy—a child—looked at his mother's eyes because she told him, kneeling on one knee to reach his level, to look at her.

'Look at me!' she repeated in an urgent whisper when he dropped his eyes to watch the moving mouth. He lifted them again and held them up while her hazel gaze toured around his face. 'You are a special boy. Do you hear me? There is nothing you cannot do.'

The boy could not keep still and moving his head to the side caused his body to twist as he looked at the other boys walking past, holding a Mama's and in some cases a Papa's hand. Some of the boys looked at him. The same ones, he noticed, looked at his Mama too. She pressed his arms against his sides and gently shook his head back around to make his eyes meet hers again. That was when she smiled at him and it was her turn to look at his mouth because something in his face had made her smile and when she smiled her eyes stopped twitching and shone. He knew he had delighted and calmed her. Something she had found in his face had satisfied her. It was easier to look into her eyes then, he even wanted to more than at other times. In her eyes was an unsolvable mystery, incomparable fascination. He smiled back at her. And when she saw his budding front teeth, something about the way she looked down while smiling made him want to clutch her shoulders and tell her: 'You are a special Mama. Do you hear me? There is nothing you cannot do.' But he did not put his hands on her. He did not say that to her. He looked aside at the other boys going by again because he knew it would draw her eyes back up from his mouth and set them moving again, and then she could finish talking and leave him to go to his new class, which he knew he had to do.

'Which of them will be my friends?' he thought. 'I don't want to be the last one to arrive,' was another thought. 'Will I ever see my mother again?' did not enter his head on the morning of his first day at school.

Inside the classroom a place was found for him to sit and to put his schoolbag that held the things he might need, except for his lunchbox and juice bottle that went on a table at the front, beside the teacher's desk, along with those belonging to all the other boys. Later he learned it was to stop him from eating during class. The idea would never have occurred to him.

It struck him as a pity that the other boys knew each other already, and knew the teacher as well. It was not because his mother had delayed outside while they all got acquainted (the ones who arrived after him were on equally familiar terms). It was because of their fathers, he suspected, because he had seen other boys' fathers meeting and seen how friendly they behaved toward one another. He could tell that their fathers had known each other in advance. They were friendly for their sons' sakes, so that their sons would get along. These boys were imitating their fathers. Inside each one's mind some image of a father lodged, as surely as a one did in his own mind.

He would say something about dogs if the chance came to speak. He knew a lot about dogs. Or something about horses, careful not to mention the knackers.

Gradually, hope that he would not have to speak at all began to burgeon. It was enough to keep track of what everyone around him was saying, and become accustomed to their appearance and how it changed slightly—surprising him—when he re-examined one while sifting for a face that he might be able talk to if he had to: the kind of face that might have a father like his own. It was a doubt-prone exercise. He could not seem to gather enough observations to be certain. One by one he disqualified each boy. Then, when none remained, he started over again.

When anticipation of the teacher reigning order began to torment the boy like hunger pain, he decided that he required an adult ally first, and then new friends later or maybe even not at all. More and more his attention was drawn to her, away from everybody else, or to the window beside his seat through which he could see headscarved women outside with despondent shoulders walking away to fill up the rest of their morning somehow. Anonymous people he felt closer to than the ones inside. Was the teacher a mother as well?

A poster hid the hand that knocked against the glass door panel of the door and brought her across from the desk where she had been reading, with a smile that the boy found encouraging at first. The door opened to the width of a blonde glossy-haired boy, and one appeared but, as if he were not late or conspicuous enough already, he immediately turned round and went out again. His small backwards body reappeared in another instant, waist bent round a collaboration between two pairs of adult hands; handed over as awkwardly as a burst sack of flour. The teacher closed the door with a foot once she had him off the ground, and held it there until she could prize his hands off the handle. Her smile never faded during the exertion, not even when the other children fell silent to better hear the screams.

*   *   *

The tribe's clicking sounds. I have to confess they made me laugh, now that I remember. It does not shame me now, in my own eyes, as much as it would have done before, to mention this fact. Why should it? In fact it honors me, in my own eyes, to have the courage to mention it so freely. It is a marvel of improvement that I have come to acknowledge and—I make no apologies for it—congratulate myself for. The clicking sounds made me laugh in the way that, later, grey pubic hairs made me laugh. It was that same kind of laugh, the nervous laugh of the stricken and alone, behind the times in his insistent stupidity.

My path was instantly mapped out before me, the investment needed, my value exposed, and the extent to which my resources had deserted me. But I stuck with the plan, I remember, until the clicking sounds no longer made me laugh (that quirk I redirected at something else). You should be aware I only allude to the African tribe here because I am reminded of, and wish to demonstrate my occasional, recurrent, stricken stupidity, something that may never leave me. That I assign improvement status to this admission might mean I am resigned to never losing my wont for unwanted laughter. All the same, those others in my company who heard me laugh, I believe, never forgot it. I must also add that, resigned or not to facts, the problem of what to do next still persists. It always has persisted.

*　　*　　*

It did not seem particularly loud to him compared with other noises, only in relation to his own silence. So long quiet he had grown unfamiliar with his own voice and when that laugh came out he instantly disowned it in disgrace. But as happens not infrequently, blame fell askew: not on the laugh that he too was startled by, but on him. Like the rest of the boys he looked around then also, but in his case it was toward the window and to the dispersing women outside that might favor him in some way in this moment of need. Or, if not now then maybe, somehow, in the long run.

But he was favored. He was favored in the short term. By some miracle he saw the dark pellet among the layer of dust coating the windowsill. Panic returned fleetingly when he considered it might simply be a chandler cast, and he was ready to accept that as fact with all the disappointment for failing to protect him from the attention his laugh had drawn. Then the panic passed. He saw it was pointed at one end, the end with fine strands of fur trapped in a tiny ferrule only visible with intense focus to the exclusion of all else. And with that level of focus he also saw the rifling all over the pellet's surface, evidence of its passage through a textured tubular channel. It was dense and, onetime, sticky. Otherwise it would have been blown away by the breeze coming through the gap in the old window.

There would be a rat in his shed in a few months, as there was every winter, and it would take a week to find and kill it. Would somebody find this school rat? He doubted it. They would not know how to go about it. They would not even know what that object was on the windowsill. With a store of private and familiar thoughts to insulate him the boy turned his face bravely back to the sideshow that was his first day at school.

The laugh encouraged the blond-haired boy and, credit to him, he did not forget the distraction that worked in his favor. It killed off the unanimous interest in his screams, which in turn killed off his screams. The calm defiance that he must have found on the laugher's face when he looked out from his nest of tousled blond hair was edifying for the laughing boy, who imbibed the hope in that gaze that gave him something more to think about besides the rat dropping: hope for a new friend. From there things fell into place, but not before our boy had almost died for his laugh during his window-search for courage, the surrounding silence ganging up on him. The rest of the boys, baying for punishment with their eyes, had been disappointed by the teacher's clemency.

THREE

My view is much better since I moved to the adjacent bed and you will have to take my word for it when I say I might never have begun writing this story had I not moved. Numerous times they said I should move, for my own benefit, appealing on behalf of the sea, neglecting to mention the crowns of the trees and the sky, and so I put them off, not wishing to be augured, not sharing their values. In the end it happened by chance. The sheets drenched from fever-sweat, I was too ill to sit on the red plastic (though quite comfortable) chair. The solution was to remove me. It took four of them, one of which is called My, the one for whom I have developed a love. They moved me to the adjacent bed while dry linen was laid down. It was soon after eight a.m. when I lay down to an altered perspective and immediately the sky's blue struck me as purer than I had ever seen it before. It could have been my first glimpse of sky such was my alarm. And then the trees that you already know about—still. The leaves were of the cleanest green I think I will ever see, each one washed by the storm that had battered the house, as I lay awake through the night, listening, wavering between bravery and cowardice.

The one I loved, and still love, My, laughed with something like wisdom when I said I would like to stay in the new bed. To kill that laugh off (it was going on far too long) I suggested I might go outside today, and sit on the veranda. But I did not stop there. I added: 'I might walk as far as the waterline', just to make sure, though I had to intention of doing either, even if permitted. It shut her up. When she realized I was putting up an act and laughed again, it was far more pleasing, and so I let it rip on, encouraging it with febrile teasing that is embarrassing to recall now, though that pleased me too at the time.

'Can you see me out there, today, my sweetest carer? Under the bare litmus sky, without your...' I adjusted my position in the bed with a sharp, vigorous hip movement that surprised both of us, '...trembling breasts for company?'

'What's the meaning of trembling breasts, Papa?'

I did not need to ask if she knew what litmus was, and so I did not, just let her laugh away, let her think she had me fooled, and I laughed along with her. Then, out of the blue, she said: 'You've had your swing of the bat, Papa,' as our laughter faded and, at that exact moment, it sounded funny, and it sounded fine. It is for moments like those, perhaps, that I love her, I think. I can listen to more when it comes from her.

*   *   *

Even children form gangs. Small children even. That is probably where it starts, one's idea of twos, threes, fours, fives, sixes and sevens and of course the precariousness of the ones. At an age when the child is so eager to learn, to emulate, there is not much hope for a one. No hope really. So there are never any ones until later. Two is the lowest a one could let itself go down to at that age, and get by. Laughing boy had made his two but if he wanted more friends he would have to jump to four, five, six... skip three.

'Never do anything as three,' his father had warned him. 'The other two can turn on you.' A fact. 'Two is better, even four is better, but best of all is one.'

There had been an almighty turbine idling out of sight, below the surface of understanding, vibrating the ground he stood upon as he listened to his father. The reverberation rose to a cringe-inducing growl, threatening an explosion. The boy braced himself. But there had been no outbreak of action. Instead his father reiterated his treasured dictum: 'Be your own man,' and the mysterious pressure had hissed away to return another day. Be your own man was alive with portent. It was best considered as a sort of prayer. It was a spiritual leap from the rest of the advice, to be treated differently. A benediction for all the advice that had gone before it.

*   *   *

Thus far, when I have the strength to walk (hobble to be precise), I go to the very edge of those lapping, dying waves on nights like this one, unobserved, when the tide is full, and the malarial mosquitoes are feeding. I swear that if I ever meet the monkey who conceived of packing repellent coils in twos, each in the other's gap, too lovingly snug to separate intact, rendered into bits in my fumbling fingers, unmountable on the aluminium barb, I will beat him with a coconut and then pour a seawater decoction of the bits into his flapping mouth, a la Khmer Rouge. Until then I will bottle my rage and hold the smoldering coil scraps in my hands during these nocturnal tide-swell visits.

Here, outside, it is all visible—all of the action that makes the noise so loud in my room. All visible in white. A ragged race, an anarchic derby of private and collaborative bows of white wash. Fatherless risings from the edge of the darkness are dropped down with bashing thumps, eggwise, from the big black hidden mother, and cracked open, the contents spread and thinned across the time-packed earth until they whisper goodbye and are absorbed. Again and again they come. Here beside me a fresh boom, and a flare of foam zips sideways and darkens into a fold of soft sea. As it goes, fifty others announce their arrival and appear in jostling impudence. On and on, thrashing the marks of what went before them, though it looks and sounds, at the instant of partum, a failure, with a better model, better only at that moment, and for a moment more. Not better over the long run, except by a few feet perhaps.

This nightly beach pounding when the tides are accommodating feed my corrupt will to live, if only to see more of these bastard deformities of water sacrificed in a time-honored cry of misguided frustration. I do not give a damn about being bitten, as such: my skin is thickened on both sides from sun and what I once had to do. I hardly itch. It is the malaria. Even that I am not so bothered about, in itself. It is a disease not without pleasant periods of delirium like any other that does not kill you. But that is my concern. It might kill me and, aside from not wishing to be augured, not knowing how I might feel about my own death as it unfolds (a thoroughgoing tragedy), my main concern is for my final love, for My. It is she who will surely suffer that I got outside without her knowledge, and that it killed me after all her efforts to keep me indoors and vital.

The fear of one more saddened heart keeps me tinkering with mosquito coils and holding the broken scraps like dim beacons as I sit on the sand staring beyond the white fringe for the silvery lights that sometimes appear, sleek as guinea fowl, far out on the surface of the water.

I am persuaded that she does not do it for the money, though doubt she would do it for no money. Always the same trouble with money, even the mere mention of it. Can't buy you love, or happiness, or time. Quite right: one needs to provide money with a catalyst. Malaria or gunshot, then put it to work. Old age will do if enough bad luck interposes: a special loss or an unusual disease. Then open up your purse (it is no good to you when you are gone) and see the abstractions crystallize into reality. For, if done correctly, the handling of money is the conservation of love. And love is all other things. My understands that. Through my money I give opportunity to her life, allow meaning to grow. Without it she would be in Sihanoukville or Phnom Penh or, heaven forbid, somewhere in Vietnam, bruising her body inside and out for different money, for her child's opportunity, her own a lost cause. Along with money I give her the aching, trembling, worthless chest that she pretends to miscomprehend. In her possession it becomes a deep well, an eternal fountain from which she draws and, like an alchemist, creates life, giving a transformed piece of myself back to me in appreciation.

A beautiful symbiosis unfolds in this secluded cove that, during certain afternoons, resembles nothing I can remember from my past, except in a painting I once saw on a woman's wall (it might have been by Monet, he will do), from far enough away to be dazed by clawing surf and molten light on flat wet sand, the sun blazing from behind my head, somewhere above the piano, the only angle from which to escape the clouds sagging over the sitting couple and make their shadows puddle. Hardly a comparison worth making, except to reveal, as best I can, the view from my new home though the bathers, rare before six, are chocolate-skinned and wire-thin, and energetic. Quite different from the couple in the painting.

Idling in the foyer of life, I and seven other independents have a chance to depart with the curiosity and fear of children facing a novel experience. Only here, in a place such as this, may one still be augured, even in our state, and feel the pleasure of refusal. Only here is it still possible. Through my glass of water I fashion memories that please me from the scrap. It is my hobby, I almost feel like saying today. Where no benefit was found in so many years, minus the first stupid ones when suffering was a passing event, I shall not find benefit hence, one might imagine. But yet I seek benefit from my memories. I tell myself I receive some benefit, the benefit of a hobby. Yes, a hobby. Mastery over my mind's flights of distress, constructions from senseless material that mandates but one simple rule: there be a before and an after with the difference amounting to mastery. Making something recognizable out of nothing or near-nothing, or out of something that is not recognizable. Making something recognizable out of something that is not recognizable. That is how I would like to describe the rule for my hobby. I always follow that rule. That is what I tell myself on a quiet day.

But all days are not the same. Sometimes when I remember what went on before (not so long before really) there is a familiar restlessness that has led me by the nose through all my spent years and I get to work. To work in earnest. To seek some benefit, not of any hobby but of real work. I set to work like a tunneler. How I loathe that word hobby! I swear I will weigh hobby's loops down with rocks and drag it by the tail of its Y through a field of landmines, shatter it once and for all, myself with it if necessary. And it will not be for the salvation of my successors, the ones that will have followed me!

That is what I feel when I am augured. When optimism seizes me so near my end, in this place where I have come to wait out the time remaining.

There is a storm at daybreak, it must be in my honor, to ruin me with hope. Ranges of turpentine mountains hammer and sluice, bulging as far as the eye can see through the gauzy spray. Septic ulcer after suppurating canker lanced and the contents spewed in my direction, drawing closer and closer. It will not take much more to reach my bed and consume me in my lair. White-variegated plots of shamrock are pushed upwards onto an edge, higher and higher, steeper and steeper, the crops uprooting and sliding to gravity, wet land bending until it can no longer support its own weight, then collapsing to smother rods of air that retouch the spent surface. Is the plowing of those fields to go on all day? I never would have believed it during last night's secret escapade.

I doze off like a baby.

I am awake. It is fully bright now, though still morning. Night and day. Not a drop of rain yet, only a slaten sky. Why not a Connemara sky, and a truculent Atlantic ocean concealing Basking sharks and immature female Blues? Because the blasting air lifting the *krama* off the table in the corner is cool, about 23°C. Cool. Did you notice that? How much I have changed! Bless me I am Asian, or African. Of the tropics at last. Equatorial. Yes I was lying about the onset of autumn and the leaves furling and all that pap. Or over-interpreting. I sometimes do if I do not get the result I am after, or so it has been remarked. It was to put myself at ease, get moving along with my story, to put me on familiar ground. The crow hopping (did I mention a crow as well?) was made up but not the few brown leaves: they were true, though maybe not deciduously shed. I do not mind admitting this to you now, now that we are on familiar terms. Maybe it is the excitement of seeing the rampaging sea and the recollection of stories I long ago memorized about villages destroyed and their people drowned by rising waters that brings forth my honest side. Stories I could not have believed true until now, looking out at this sea.

Before My arrives to close the door, sand, fine as white paper, finds my bed, lips and eyes. The mosquitoes are hiding somewhere saying their prayers. I ask My to leave it ajar and permit the air some free passage.

'It's a day for you Papa,' she says (she knows me so well), 'but maybe not for them. The sand will give them pneumonia.' We both know the other six are weaker than me.

'And?' I do not say but rather: 'It doesn't matter, the air is getting in anyway.' 'And the sand too,' I also do not add because My likes to feel wiser than the person she is speaking to. It is woven into her soul, a reason why I am drawn to her. Opposites.

Higher still the tilting rows of sea, creaming into waves farther out, driving harder, more disorderly, impatiently butting against each other for a shortcut to shore. The mainsail of a small craft flutters around an exposed rock that lies far out, half way to the horizon. It is shaped like a square tooth. Beside it, I know, is the bud of a smaller neighbor, capable of breaking the surface of the sea's gum on calmer days. But not today. Geysers of spume bullet over the tiny island and I wonder what grounds the light craft has for passing so close to peril. Curiosity perhaps, or sympathy; it looks all but done for in this sea (the island, that is, not the switching sail that resembles an active quill). Then I wonder what grounds it has for being out on this type of sea at all. And in turn I wonder . . . but I stop myself before I wonder about the grounds for everything. I have not the time any more for that. I must be selective if I am to be rid of things.

I lean forward with purpose from the pillow and open my legs like a younger man. My rubs my back, not merely with a hand but using most of her arm. From shoulder blades to coccyx and over again. That is how close she is against my side. My back is hers, her imagination's womb I fancy. But I must return to the story I am telling, return to gangs, while the storm permits it.

FOUR

Days before the autumn term ended the boy was accused of being in a gang run by Stanislaus Platt who had chubby hands and performed Chinese burns, and he no longer thought about his mother being gone. For the gang charge he was caned on the palms and ordered to 'desist'. By agreeing to desist (what else could he do with the cane so warm and ready?), he inadvertently admitted to the spurious accusation and justified his punishment. This admission, he observed, induced in the eyes of his caner (the mistress) a turn from hostility to affection. Later she would discover that he would sometimes stay silent rather than risk a wrong response. But that is all to come. Alert as a mongoose he was to become as well, and that too in good time.

Here is what is important about the end of the first school term: it ended differently for the boy than for the others. On the first day of the school holidays he suddenly felt older, like an old man whose friends and family have all died. There was no good in telling himself they would come back in January. At his current rapid rate of aging he would be dead by then himself if he did not conquer this sense of perishability that had mysteriously appeared. The next time he saw his classmates—if he ever saw them again (his doubt was genuine)—he would have to hide something and start over, even if it were only his fear of not seeing them again and the enfeebling relief when he did.

Time yawned on that day while he sat alone in the now familiar classroom practicing his handwriting and coloring in outlines from a vast pad that, although he enjoyed the final result, seemed to be pointlessly hard work. As for the handwriting template, the letters were garishly large. The challenge he felt was artificially inflated with scale. Nobody writes giant letters except sign writers, as his father would have told him.

Now empty, the classroom smell previously hidden under a live atmosphere of soap, tire-smoke, sherbet, shoe-polish, cola, butter and skin-dried urine emerged to claim the air with a different but related odor that struck him as holy. When he put his nose to a greasy desk panel he found the source, until he sniffed the waxy floor and it was there too. It also came off the blackboard and the chalk dust he chased along the groove in the ledge with a fingertip that went purple, white and eggshell-blue. It was even in the gloopy glass and sash wood of the draughty windows. It was only the glossy stippled walls that held a different, bland smell, and they felt clammy.

The same smell must have been here every morning during term. He would discern it in future, he knew, so long as there was a future. A compost of living scents had been compacted, day upon day, year after year. All organic matter reduced to one irreducible and volatile substance that contained a biopsy of every boy that had ever been in that room. The instant he made that discovery, it were as though he could feel the other boys' presence when he breathed through his nose. Something of his classmates was surely there. One by one he placed each of them back in the room. When he sat at their desk he not only felt the presence of that boy, he became that boy. He learned something about him that he had not known before. He knew how that other boy saw the rest of the boys, how he saw the teacher, and what he saw when he stared up at the blackboard.

Moving through the chilly classroom, sitting at each desk, he had time to make himself every boy's friend. He came closer to each of them than if they had actually been there. Thus our boy passed the morning hours of that first day of the holidays, daydreaming, and coloring with the design scheme of the friend whose desk he happened to be sitting in. Writing with one boy's clumsiness or another's elegance.

'Lunch, Eoin.' The mistress announced, without shouting, calling him by his Christian name from her office down the corridor in her term-soprano that travelled the distance between the rooms effortlessly. From that day, he realized, some woman other than his mother would henceforth utter his name relentlessly, and he would have to get used to that.

Together they sat in her office, warmed by a portable fire, where the whiff of heated milk poured over Nescafe and sugar granules spun his heart with a guilty yearning, and they ate bouncy salad sandwiches and King crisps and Eoin was given a Big Time for himself.

'Would you like a sip?' She seemed to be bending the rules with her offer, tilting her mug temptingly but, he thought, then what? Another sip? A sip each day from her cup? Finally a full cup? What next to bind them together?

'No thanks,' he said, and took a sip of his Mi-Wadi to show her he was self-sufficient, like the Australians. Eoin's uncle lived in Australia. They had met once when he came back for a visit after twenty years away. For Eoin it was love at first sight. He wore mallard-green trousers and tawny shirts and smoked Golden Virginia from a pond-green pouch. He liked to have his sandwiches made-to-order from the delicatessen. 'No,' he had said in a nasal whistle, Aussie accent to go with it, his nose hooked and twisted from a fall or a fist in the reform school Eoin heard called Daingean, 'the snakes are nothing to warry about.' Eoin believed him when he said that they slithered off at the slightest tremor from human footsteps. That had been the only concern holding him back. His Mama had wanted to take him, just she and Eoin, to visit her brother in Melbourne. It had been their dream, his dream now. He must not forget it. It had become a serious business, dreaming. Much more serious for a one.

After lunch on that first day of the holidays the mistress resumed her work and Eoin went back to giving himself up to his classmates' ghosts. The shifting clock hands eventually made them unwelcome and the mistress called out his name again, and they left in her getaway car. At least that is how he thought of it from the way she drove. In their wake, jangling keys and thudding doors and clopping bootsteps all a-mingle and echoing in the dusky, holy air.

FIVE

Jump with Eoin now into a different car. It is seven and a half years later. He is nervous but the excitement is pleasing. Every second crackles with the promise of dramatic disruption of life and order. A germinating spirit of detachment promises to lift him out from, and above, the doubt-world and into a clearing of calm serenity. As it grows he notices how his lumpen anxiety is fragmenting into smaller, fortifying grains that scratch and roughen every nook and cranny inside his body. His fear is being reduced to a mild and pleasurable irritability.

In the front passenger seat, he does not consciously move a muscle apart from his eyes. But he seems to himself to be vibrating. Through his body's vibration he draws confidence that from his still state he is capable of launching movement of dumbfounding and error-free deftness (when people talk of the immortality of youth, I believe they refer to moments like these).

The man next to him drives carefully. Tom Jones is turned up high and when Gerry sings along with Tom for a bar (never more than a bar) he locks his exceptionally long arms against the wheel and tucks his shaven chin into the V of his open shirt-collar. Then his voice fades out as he makes a catty pan round to the side window, as though something outside has distracted him. He frequently glances at Eoin but Eoin does not glance back. It could be a test. He is still in training, and doing awfully well. Gerry wears glasses and looks like a schoolteacher, of the firm but fair variety. He seems to assume his own authority. He can get away with murder on account of this appearance.

Slow-witted people move dazedly about on the streets outside with guileless vulnerability. Big babies, Eoin thinks of. Fish cut off in a draining lagoon, their world tinier than his, much tinier. That is how it all appears to him that evening as a wedge of gold is pressed out from the western rim of a bruised and cloud-battered sky. Still too early, Gerry says, and pulls off the road into a quiet lane he knows well. He cuts the engine, lowers Delilah a notch. With the car pointing west, Gerry reaches his gibbon arms into the back seat and retrieves a Toblerone and a flask of sweetened tea. Gerry cannot sing in a stationary car so he talks.

Eoin has a sense that Gerry values him. He thinks he knows what for but does not allow himself to be too sure. This evening, however, he allows himself to be less unsure than usual. It is his arms and hands. Other things too, sure, or maybe sure, but above all Eoin's long arms and his steady hands. Gerry said so that afternoon in his garage after a flawless rehearsal. Flawless, that is, as rehearsals go: the real thing always threw up a surprise, even if that surprise consisted in no surprise.

'Once', Gerry mentions, 'three of us headed out after weeks of preparation. Driving home afterwards one got strange. Started talking about going back and resetting the timer (that time we used a clock) to morning or some "better" time. He was turning Russian. "Do you want it stopped altogether?" I said to him casually. I had no intention of going back of course. I had known all along, you see. The third man was confused by the Russian. But I wasn't. I had my proof during the final run. As soon as the live jelly appeared I diagnosed over-eagerness. And what it might foreshadow. It was too late to get somebody new (*it was too late, Eoin understands, for Gerry to admit that either he had had doubts all along, or that he had not*), so I armed himself with certain precautions.'

Eoin listens to the slow, solemn narration. The car windows catch the tea-steam. Cool milky droplets bead the threaded cup-rim, which near to Eoin's nose smell of rainsoaked clothes left lying. The end brick refuses to give. Eoin pushes the other way and the peak topples over.

'Give it to me,' says Gerry, a hint of nicotine–deprived irritation in his tone. His bunched pointy fingertips gouge into the valley of foil and a piece and a half of Toblerone comes off in one continuous action. Eoin takes it from him and gnaws. Gerry goes on.

'He wanted to take us to Saint Peter. Then leave us two stranded at the gates while he marched on in. Or so he thought.'

Gerry's black eyebrows jump above the lens-frame.

'See, I had him set the timer before we left. That was his part. Before any connections were tied. Then, I had him do watch. Away from the kettle. While we did the arming. That made him aware that I knew. Thinking about that kept his mind occupied.'

Eoin takes in this story appreciatively, it goes well with Tom Jones; together it binds his concentration at a steady pitch and draws him in closer to Gerry and their work. And so the time passes until nightfall: Gerry bestowing knowledge, Eoin learning. He does not ask what happened to the Russian in the end (for there had to have been an end) and Gerry does not volunteer the information. Probably, he would have, gladly even, if Eoin had asked. But something tells Eoin that it is not important. Or that it is less important than other things, than the positive things. Somehow, Gerry registers this inward discipline, and what is sometimes known as trust deposits like silt a tombolo between this man and boy. Quiet lovely.

*   *   *

Cowboy boots were the fashion then for women, and large noses with bony facets, particularly the downward break that certain noses, though unbroken, have just below the saddle; something both equine and leonine, Arabic and African, about that angular proboscis that disobeys the beauty rules and casts new light on ugliness. To finish, the bridge is drawn down in a wide V, stretching and raising the outer corners of the eyes. Eyes and nose strained in a taut sculpture. There were cigars too or cigarillos, some quite thick, and all chocolaty and rummy as they burned fresh; grassy when stale. Yet when they are fresh they can never become stale, says the nose. We have not done with the boots: reptilian leather, naturally sequined, in pale tones with a blackened tip, heel and shaft-collar appears to have worked best. There were no spurs, though I dare suppose on account of the furniture, and the cost of repairing punches in hardwood flooring and chair legs. But for all I know it could have been because of the damned noise spurs make.

The mistress looked younger in her cowboy boots, with her cigarillo. Her hair, richly woven into a *brioche* during term, now hung around her shoulders. Girlish clips exposed her rectangular forehead. With every puff of smoke fired from the edge of her mouth, out through the gap in the car window, she seemed to transfigure one more part of herself into a foreign object. Her knees, Eoin noticed, no longer sought one another relentlessly but slackened apart on the car seat, occasionally twitching together as if in a dreamworld of their own. But these changes are as difficult to detail as the new expression in her face, the new smile.

When Eoin looked at her he began to fall off the edge of a precipice, or so it felt, until he rescued himself by looking away. What else did he get from that smile? Sympathy? Yes. And something else too. Much else. But how deceiving to guess now at something like 'inviting'. No, nothing I can think of will do. All I shall say is that in the mistress's smiling face, as they drove away from the school to where Eoin would spend his first night away from home, there was a promise of surprise. Only many years later did he consider that the mistress saw something similar in his own face. Don't we all love surprises, not least seven-year-old boys and certain women?

*   *   *

The news breaks on Gerry's TV the same night. Relief sweeps over them both firstly, then exhilaration comes for Eoin. Gerry looks at all the faces at the scene to pick up additional information, the real news. The driver of the car worked nights. The explosion occurred as he turned onto Forest Hill Road on his way to work. He was taken to the Royal Infirmary and at the last report was in critical condition.

'He will die so,' says Gerry and that seems to be enough to say.

'God bless him,' he then adds, and Eoin is reminded that bravado is wrong; violence is to be used only when other means of self-expression have failed. It must not become a pleasure, or even easy. Gerry's solemnity leaves Eoin in limbo, not sure how or even if to broach their success, and unable to switch his thoughts to anything else. There are some onion rings left in the nest of paper. He takes one and with the other hand he reaches for the coke can. He shakes it. It is empty. He knew it was empty, but he drains a drop by tilting his head far back because the extreme movement helps him not to think, and he sucks air from the can because any sound that he can make brings him relief during one of Gerry's noisy silences.

SIX

It is summertime, the season for thinking of autumn. Greenfly infest the tree where Eoin waits for night to become morning on a Fermanagh roadside. In the darkness he imagines he is being bitten. The tree, a nice broadleaf (a sycamore he thinks) has a dense crown and he will have to strip away some of the sappy branches to see the whole porch across the horse meadow. This he could do by night. But he will wait for the first glaze of dawnlight, as close to the time as he dares in case something goes wrong. In case he is being watched. In case he drops something. In case it becomes windy, or it rains and the branches hang in a new fashion. In case it disrupts his concentration is the main reason why he does nothing, once wrapped in tree limbs, until first light.

He could happily sit there forever, he imagines: a dangerous monkey with a Cadbury's Tiffin and an oiled rifle. Brass, walnut, steel and copper-coated lead. The mute complexity of what he bears, its autumnal beauty, unhesitant precision and loyal long-lived smell of fresh manhood pegs him to the life he is now leading. It allows him the gift of mastery.

Nobody can take his marksmanship from him. Nobody can beat him at this game. He is the best shooter they have. Never needs to be closer than two hundred yards, usually works nearer three, routinely five with the scope. But that does not matter; he does not miss, that is all one needs to know. He killed a ewe, dropped her flat like a sack of cement from eight hundred in Kilbride as the last jeep was being loaded, the rest of the convoy already over the brow of the *bóithrín*. It was off-range and the bullet whizzed across a hikers path. He could have been locked up (the thought curled his toes an hour later, when his adrenaline waned). Blonde boy, watching through binoculars, saw the animal collapsing. Eoin saw only the flock scatter and the speck of his target remain stationary. There had been no wind and it was a downhill shot. Nevertheless.

It rains. The sky blushes black-orange and drops gush in showers between the tree and the house, spattering the flat leaves, shushing the meadow grass, stirring the horses to whinny and snort. But the rain comes without any wind and so it does not feel cold. Passing cars, the few that there are, hose standing water from the asphalt in crescendo, decrescendo.

'If only they knew,' Eoin thinks, as the headlights build and the taillights fade. Rills of rainwater trickle onto his thighs and shoulders but it is mainly dry inside his hide and, internally, soundless. The branches make no sound. The stillness of these living limbs seems like a sign of acquiescence, even approbation, supporting his weight, as they do, one of them his rifle case. The man, who would leave his house to go to his problematic work as he did most days, had not planted this tree. It had anteceded him. They had been neighbors up to today, the man and this tree that grew at the end of a diagonal firing line from his doorstep across the meadow. They had lived side by side in peace. The tree, silent and still, had always only observed (if a tree could be said to observe). It had done no harm to anybody through a willfulness to inhabit some other place or to act. It had simply stayed where it was, and lived. Lived simply. The man may even have been fond of the tree. Somewhere in his mind, as he lifted his morning eyes to the sky for reassurance, an impression of this tree must have become etched; a part, however small, of the daily affirmation of the activity that he felt urged to perform by a mysterious force, the work that had made up a significant part of his life until today.

The man, a father, was older than Eoin. He was of Eoin's father's generation. Men of his father's age were a little like trees, but in a peculiar way. Although still and stubborn they wanted, too much, to move and to act. They were rogue trees, unlike the generation before them, the grand- and great grand-people who were, Eoin supposed, though he had never known any of them, more like the tree Eoin was hiding in. Placid things. That is why they lived to be grand and great and grey and grog-nosed. Modern fathers were a colder lot. They felt nothing for others, least of all their sons. They rampaged. They ransacked. They had faith in, and enjoyed, the regular violence they committed, violence unto others, and thought they were untouchable, that nobody else could match them.

They were nearly correct. Almost nobody could match them. But there were a few that could. Those few could outstrip them. For those few, violence had become clarified. It was absolute. Something Eoin's father and his peers only bluffed.

Sufficient was enough for Eoin, he had discovered. If he had enough of something, he believed with tremendous certainty, without any particular object in mind, he would never seek more than that feeling. To be left alone to work in a secluded corner, like this, shooting every day. There he could happily get by on what was sufficient for life: food and a purpose. An arboreal creature. An orang-utan. How was he, himself, destined to die? Nobody shot snipers. Orang-utans did not kill orang-utans. Perhaps he would be toppled against the ground one day.

'You don't hear the bullet that kills you,' were his father's words. But you hear the one that misses you. And if you do, Eoin knew, it would make you freeze. A travelling explosion, the molecular crack of splitting air and, buried inside it, the nascent thump. It did only one thing, and it did it every time, always reproducibly. Parting air in search of concealment and deceleration. It left behind quite a different sound, a dull boom like a mine in a bog that made one's ears ring. That is what the cotton pellets were for. Eoin knew the sound of a .303 bullet at both ends of its journey. The end that was more deafening, the one more paralyzing, on account of which a second shot, if needed, was possible if one were quick enough. He would reload instinctively and take first pressure before re-sighting the dead, wounded or missed target, and fire immediately if necessary, keeping in mind a third was a badge of disgrace.

Dawn fatigue he had heard it called, the sudden weariness that comes with the greyish light. They said it was the slow unveiling of the world you had been anticipating through the darker hours only to find it, somehow, disconcertingly different. Others said it was due to a change that was too prolonged, too dense, and they called it adjustment fatigue. For hours one dwells in a state of mental preparedness, having come to terms with all that can be seen and heard in the environment, even smelled. But that is only part of it. The rest of the preparedness comes from extrapolations to future minutes and hours and the events one expects to unfold.

Actions can be rehearsed in the mind, anywhere, at almost any time, until even the thought is automatic. But can one extrapolate black to grey? Water-trough to foal? Grey, that was black, to yellow a hundred times and at once? Can one imagine a shadow is a bird feeder and then catch up with the small arms and nightdress that are stretching to sprinkle sunflower seeds before breakfast? Can you ignore the uncertainty allowed by a growing light that reveals a creature, but not yet enough to know whether it is a rabbit, a stout or a squeezing hand? Is it better not to know in case it is something else entirely, something one could never imagine? Are you not surprised by your uncertainty? And what about that sullen mound that darkens so much of the field, that you stared at more often than the house itself even though you had decided what it was? Where you unsure after all? You needed more light to convince you it was rotting sward stretched over with plastic, lashed down with ropes and tires. That it was not an operations tent, darker inside than your own tree, hiding superior eyes to yours. Can you extrapolate the relief of knowing for certain it is not?

A hasty clearing away of ragged and spent rain clouds opens the sky to the sun's first colors and Eoin fights the leaping consideration that the gentle scrolling of this one day is indistinguishable from all the others, as far as the sun is concerned; as far as everything he can see with his own eyes is concerned. But was he not about the make it different? The sun would hang and burn and not flinch while he changed the pattern of the world. One second before, it would shine. BANG! One second later, it would shine. Or would it? Would it shine steadily for Mr. John Love too? Might the sun not protest? If something were wrong would it not show him, go into retreat behind the Slieve Beagh? That is where Mr. Love would look when his confused head reeled with uncommon wakefulness to his surroundings in the final second that expands to eternity as he travels through time, surprised at how alive he is, so close to death. He will surely try to turn to the sun for reassurance when his body absorbs the thump. What details will appear to him then and for the first time in his life?

One might say he is merely searching for the sky in which case I ask: what is the sky only a diffusion of sun? Who looks at a clear sky without noting the sun's position? Will he not see in the sun some twitch of revulsion, recognition of what is happening, representing the fleeting possibility of complete derailment of the natural system thereafter to terrify him? Surely he will hope to find, in a stable sun, comfort that everything else is going on as usual, can get along without him. That what is about to happen to him (what is in fact well underway) is nothing to worry about, a glitch too minor to trouble the daily journey of the sun which, he will correct himself, is really the journey of the earth he is about the die upon. And he will hope to discover that all his problems are minor, after all, and that when he ends they too will end, and that will be a great thing. That is what he will seek: his final discharge granted by the sun.

The morning light is steady when Eoin at last asks himself if he would have some regret if he were Mr. Love and some orang-utan were about to send him a similar message of understanding. His answer, No, dispels any remaining dawn fatigue he may have been feeling. The rifle when disturbed seems to awaken inside the case on which slothful greenfly, intoxicated by gun oil, are caught unawares. He easily clears them away.

SEVEN

They are building a new house, expanding. They are using my money I suspect. You should see what they use for scaffolding. Branches dredged from the bottom of the river. Each one is straightish on the whole but gnarled like a helix. Nobody who gets up on those sticks weighs more than 120 pounds, and they constantly move to distribute their weight. But then I have seen the branches used to hold concrete forms too, so my wonder remains valid: the twistedness appears to make them weak but could it in reality do the opposite. It is a possibility I have to allow.

By day I hear their sounds. I follow this discordant orchestra of clanging and buzzing, the generator's tapping. The cool smell of wet concrete sometimes drifts across to excite me. I have watched the workers pass along the sand, shouldering their bundles of scaffold-staves like the best cuts from some elegant beast. Evenings, when the noise ends I watch out for the surf invasion and feel some of their selfsame satisfaction, as though I too had converted my life's time and energy into something I will later seek another, longer-lasting satisfaction from, at various future dates that for now are vague and unimportant. The work is deliberately slow, I sense. All the better. I am enjoying it. I am in no rush for them to finish either. I am not going anywhere. *Arbeit macht frei.*

Later, at night-time, when they have gone home to their families and

I go to the waterline on the night tide, it is from their dusty and sweat-soaked bodies I try to see the water. It works, at least a little, a little more each night as I edge nearer the sea flames and enjoy their imagined satisfaction. I often wonder what they make of me, when I return their passing glances. I doubt I will ever know, or come even close to imagining correctly, though I constantly try.

The other day two of them, heads and necks wrapped in their maroon *kramas,* one commenting, both laughing, spoke in reference to me. I am quite certain. Afterwards, I cudgeled my thoughts to put myself in their place, each separately, and tried to conjure the impression the inside of my room made on them with its faint traces of life. The inhabitants of the room less gregarious than a covey of flightless pullets. Did they settle on some reason why my coevals and I might have wound up here? Is it a better one than mine? Was their image, looking in, an inversion of mine, looking out: of hydration and activity, sweeping vistas and boundless possibilities? There seems little doubt about that much. But did they see more than opposites? I fancied by their manner they were not as surprised, not as horrified as I might have been, had I been them.

But hard as I tried to be them I could not arrive at the attitude I witnessed. I tried again and again to re-interpret, shifting around the few ideas I could conceive of entering the minds of young Cambodians, indeed young men in general. Nevertheless it was, at last and comfortingly, more instinctive than what I was not prepared to do: admit to myself it did not matter one way or another.

Thus the time passed that day in a neighborly spirit. Those workers, indigenes, are my real neighbors now. They are the citizenry of my final land. I am a citizen too, a part of that citizenry. I have always tried my best to get along with my neighbors, whoever they may be. I have a new chance to try that again, you see. A rare chance. All I have to do is reach out to them and (you might raise an eyebrow) try to understand them without trying to make them understand me. It is just a little work I must do each day to make it possible.

But some days, like today, that little seems quite a lot, almost too much. Quite suddenly I can become consumed by a futility so great that no will can drive it away. That much I have come to dread. I must wait. But it is not simple waiting, as I suggested earlier, as children wait, as mothers wait, as fathers wait, as dogs wait for something to happen that they know will happen. How I wish it were. That beautiful waiting: plump with preserved action, with impatience for plans and visions of a different future to unfold. Waiting is the wrong word, but if I say hesitating that will be worse, yet there is something hesitant in it. I will say stop and you will understand a bit more; I must stop everything, and allow time to elapse, events to occur around me. Then, some time later, I will unstop. I will know what to think . But that is too presumptuous: when I stop I never expect to unstop, to know what to think; unstopped I always fear the next stopping.

*   *   *

With a smooth swoosh the mistress's boots slipped off. Lamplight sparkled and plum varnish showed through the nylon as she kneaded an arch with her knuckles. Eoin's eyes grappled for images in the sitting room to anchor his thoughts. A tree twinkled in the corner. The room had fir-green carpet and smelled of pine needles and turf smoke; the cleanest smell he had ever known also contained a tinge of sweet perfume that he imagined hung at higher altitude or in some secret corner of the house in purer, denser form.

But here I must pause to erase the white-sailed boat from my mind. I mention it again. Why is it still there, days later, while I spin out my longing like warm toffee? It threatens to cut across my ordered strands of thought and tangle what I have meticulously laid out. I will not start again. I cannot. I have given this story everything so far, I swear to you. Up to this point I have never thought I could do better (and I did ask myself at every moment: are you sure that this happened? Quite like this? Sure?). Only once when I confessed about the crows and the autumn leaves did I reach this point before now. But then I confessed to you, did I not? Even though in Ireland it was bound to have been quite similar to how I described it. At least I believed it to be exactly as I described it, which is the important thing. Just because I am not there now does not mean autumn is not showing its face once more; that the curious crows are not interrogating fallen husks, jabbing into the mud their beaks. I tend to test myself. To an unwholesome extent I am sure you would say, if you knew the full extent.

It is this doubt that I keep mentioning, dropping in here and there to my story. I want to tell you that doubt replaces the people I wish were closer to me, could have been closer to me one time. It floods that gap with a pliable material. Then I spend my time, my life, working out a way to ford the flood of doubt and get my understanding across safely, quite certain none will return to me, that in this way my work is in vain, if mutual understanding be my aim.

But what is my aim, or anybody else's if we are honest about it, if not mutual understanding? When I contemplate my erection I want to describe it to you via the sound of certain music but I have not the time or wherewithal to describe one of Chopin's nocturnes, the mention of which I wanted to omit altogether because I must be selective, yet it is a part of the story I wish to tell. Even at my age it happens without warning and interrupts my thoughts, demands special attention. It is a fair size, by the way, just in case you think I am misleading you into thinking I am a man without pride. That pride I speak of, it too still raises its mast without warning. But I do not want to waste time with pride any more. If it reoccurs then it will have been due to my failure to achieve one small aim: to tell this story without pride.

When I saw the boat the other morning, out in the storm, I stopped my writing (because of the right-sided curve my left hand has difficulty) and for a few moments as I lay with both knees raised beneath the sheet, masked by the L-shaped bookcase, where I keep my candles and mosquito coils, looking out at the white sail I slowly felt the movement as if I were the pilot of that reckless boat. What would I have done had My come to my side then? Now, thinking of her catching me in that state it is easy to suppose it would have been shameful. But, during the height of it, you have to take my word that I would have wanted her to witness my pleasure, and my wonder (they are both intertwined). I would have wanted her to know everything beneath the surface: what I was doing, and how much physical, guilty pleasure it can sometimes give one like me to be alive.

I delayed until my hunger demanded more and at last I shook for a few long terrifying seconds that I had known best in my childhood. Afterwards, I had only regrets. My doubts were torrential, my aims laughable. The boat began to annoy me, flitting as it did past what I was now more interested in: that bleak island, non-descript and mulish. Something so dreary yet so prevailing that a short while ago was so incidental. I wanted that boat smashed upon it in payment for my pleasure. I wanted to talk to the black rock. Who else should I turn to in this matter? Who else was involved but the boat, that island and me? We three. I had betrayed the island, now I would make it up by betraying the boat. Yes the island: in the long run it was better than the boat. Why? Because it would never go away. Yes, that is it. It would stay there, for me to see, for as long as I could look. Disloyal bastards we are all the same! Who else would have the faintest interest? To whom else should I try to explain the unexplainable? Failure or failure to know, those are the options.

I pull myself off again, and again without My knowing, at the memory of that morning during writing these words, as you will have no doubt correctly guessed. We are always a little more circumspect after the first time, are we not? Keep a little of ourselves aside to monitor the event for posterity. Oh did you not know? Those second times you equate with first times because they are the first you speak of.

Anyway, it does not matter how you enumerate things. You face the same trouble in the end.

*   *   *

'What more do you want? Hands up, please, if you think you can answer.'

'Nothing, I have everything.'

Correct. But unacceptable. You must list things, at least one thing, so I can discuss it with you and show you its other side, the side you do not know, the flaw in the thing you think you want. How do you fancy that? I, teaching you, that you want for nothing really, that you have everything already. I, teaching you, to identify what you really want and then to recognize that you have it. It sounds like a game and, depending on my mood, it can appear so. But do not be presumptuous. This is serious. Either way you must participate. Or you will die from the toxin I blended into the words of the previous section of this story, absorbed through your eyes and now running amok quietly inside your body. There is no cure; they do not even believe such a toxin exists because they cannot detect it. It is activated by a particular pattern of words. Read in a certain sequence this toxin becomes lethal. So sorry to speak of this now, so late, but I am sure you can understand why I had to wait until you had enough exposure to kill you before telling you about it.

Not to worry, it is not all doom and gloom. There is an antidote, but you will not find it anywhere else but here, in the next section of my story. I have engineered the antidote, too, into the words. That is all I will say for now. I will tell you when you have had enough of the antidote to save your life. I will tell you when you are healthy again. I will tell you when your life is no longer in mortal danger, when it has been rescued, because you will not know otherwise. All your presumptions, whatever they be, will be wrong. I will see to that. I mean I will know that. Sorry. . . you see I am using that word again, whimpering again. I use it because I love you, to use the other important word for drawing people near to us when all they want to do is run away from our cruelty. I am not a cruel person; it just seems that way sometimes. I am a good person. You must trust me. Do you understand? Trust me when I tell you these things, the way I trust you. If you do not then everything will turn out badly for both of us. But especially for you. And that is the last thing I want, because I love you and, believe me, want to help you to get out of this mess you are in. To hell with it: the mess we are both in! You and I together. Now you see how honest I am. How much we have in common.

*　　*　　*

Steam clouds billowed upwards from the tumbling water as Eoin stood by naked and waiting. He had never taken a bath with his mother as far as he could remember. But there had never been a tub as large as this one; that, at least, was a fact. Another fact was he had never seen his mother's cunt. Or her nipples. He did not tell the mistress because her behavior seemed to indicate that she thought he had. Knock, knock went an air bubble in a buried pipe that his father had trained him to identify and a moment later, as expected, the sputtering and rasping to his relief. The mistress added an arc of indigo to the waterfall that instantly erupted, upon contact, into white quivering foam, and turned the steam spearmint. The water she lowered her body into looked scolding. As she put her arms behind her, straight down, two hollowed wishbones appeared at her neck and turned her into a child and him into a man, a little man. She purred as the water rose to cover her sallow goose bumps with their ant-antennae down. Tongues of black hair caught the foam and fell slick against her neck.

After a glance at his clothes pile to ensure that the stain, like crayon, was hidden inside the folded underpants Eoin extended a leg into the bath and said nothing about the icy burn. His scrotum, firm and crimped as a walnut husk, felt a fleeting lick of fire. But the immediate sting on the tip of his penis and around the roll of skin persisted and made him want to urinate urgently until he was well beneath the foam, not sure whether he had done or not.

When she opened her eyes and stopped humming, and told him to turn around, that she would wash his back, he was so surprised to hear her speak that he jumped back up and slipped. Though he knew it was just a harmless little slip he wanted to cry. She caught one of his arms and, steadying him with her other hand on his backside, she eased him down against her knee and in between her flexed legs. At the touch of her hands that urge to cry merely intensified, but the motive had entirely changed. What beckoned to him was a cry that would crack open the thousands of confused words rushing forward, mashed together into a clay boulder, roasted to an exterior glaze: a cry of transfer of ownership to inaugurate a new mother. A birth cry, potentially. But somehow it only reached to the soft palate of his mouth. Then it went back down to someplace inside of him. Gone, almost without a trace.

EIGHT

Unplugging a drain hole at the equator, the water sinks without any vortex. It can make one's world fall apart, being so simple and inconsequential. At an abandoned school where I saw water gurgle and stagnantly sink I was reminded of the lethal jungle swamps, leech-infested, hidden by floating plant-carpets, and for the first time in years I discovered I could be afraid (I could not comprehend their role, whichever way I considered those swamps). Later that same day I found out that what we had been calling pig, the animal that trod on the mine the previous night and fed us, was something else. After seeing the water drain I could no longer condone vague appellations; it had not been pink, it had been black; it had not grunted or squealed, it had merely breathed heavily; its fat was not sweet but slightly bitter. And the monkeys, they were not monkeys as I had known monkeys. They did not have zoo-monkey eyes. They had goat-eyes, milky blue. And who were the owners of those sounds they told me came from birds? They were not the sounds of crows or pigeons or sparrows. I saw none of those kinds.

Before that day, I realized, I had accepted all this strangeness on faith, something I might have continued to do so had it not been for the water in the drain. Suddenly I missed swirling water with such force that, back then, I believe I allowed was for somebody I thought I loved, or for my country, the one I had wished to go back to, with its sweet grunting pigs and murders of crows, the monkeys in cages with brown eyes. But I wonder had I not merely yearned for one simple thing, the normal draining of water, which I never doubted I would find everywhere, even in a place like this, until that day. I could hardly act without remembering the water and how shocking it was to be disturbed by a matter so minor. From there I saw each of the objects that made up my day as mysteries laden with disturbing potential, if I were only to become more aware of them. An accretion of those mysteries began to slow my brain. And here is where I fail most to describe my predicament: it was as if one thousandth part of what I allowed myself to see and do each day I became convinced was a single thought away from shocking me out of existence if I re-examined it. 'Do I want to cease in Africa?' I asked myself, 'die like a Congolese despite being a foreign indigene?'

From the shock of the water I began to appreciate the unimaginable danger that now lay all about me, barely hidden from sight. The threat of mambas sent me into a peculiar state of dreaminess, from which what I knew or did not now at any moment was reduced to a question of contemporaneous courage. If I wanted to know just one more little thing I had only to part the leaves to see a pair of reptilian eyes. No surprise that it became increasingly difficult to keep up with the others and to do my job.

But who has the answers to your questions? The jungle's damp nights chilled bones at higher altitude and though other game was scarce, there were gorillas for us to eat. The three bullets needed to stop the first one we ate (one in the massive chest, two in the back) were a source of interest to my colleagues, and not his eye. Was it the beautiful agate marble and how it came to be there that interested me most, or the sight of everybody else in my world denying my observation? Maybe they did this deliberately, I thought, to isolate me. I could not be certain, knowing to where an inquisition on the fake eye would lead us all.

The bullets they knew all about: 0.5 caliber. Where they entered they also knew: stomach and lung, liver, heart and trachea. And they knew arthropods. They knew roasted gorilla fat. But about prostheses in general, and the people who attached them to wild animals, they were superstitiously ignorant. If I had said anything about the eye I would have had to mention the water next. Then who knows what danger I would have hailed upon myself, as well as them. One of them would have had to conclude our discussion, eventually, with a clarification of *our* understanding, or else I with *mine own*, in either case exposing by how much what we were doing was wrong: all of it. The damage would have been irreversible.

One must be stupid at a given time in a gang for it to keep on running. That is one of the problems: knowing whose turn it is and taking our turn when it arrives, with alacrity. It can be very subtle. I gave an opinion on the third bullet (the fatal one) though it held no interest for me except for the idea that the gorilla had never heard it.

NINE

'It's cuntish. If I say "Da" I burden myself with being a son. What do I call him? "Papa"?'

'Poxbottle. Don't call him anything. Don't mention him.'

Blonde-boy, who was once given the name Aaron by someone who will never appear in this story, and Eoin are stretched out on the opposing benches of a picnic table. They are outside a remote pub in Kerry. There is a smell of toasted sandwiches. Through the supple trees that line the road they can see the barren brown land rising, and beyond the ridge of McGillycuddy's Reeks the jutting pyramidal peak of Carrauntoohil in faded navy. It is late July. It is after eight but the sun is still bright.

'If I have to say anything about him to people I say "father". Makes him seem like a holy man. Then I can break my bollocks laughing. I could be talking about any old bastard who wears black and feels entitled to your soul.'

'Or wears green and owns your soul.'

They laugh together, stomach muscles contracting and pulling them up off the bench. They have to hold the tabletop or brace an arm against the ground to keep from falling off the plank. When Eoin finally stands up he experiences that peculiar weightlessness that comes when you discover a pleasure where once there was only fear. It is a conqueror's moment. In another moment it is gone.

Across the road a green Mercedes pulls into the small car park. A vigilant but slovenly man gets out and looks up and down, puts his hands in the pockets of his trousers. Around his elbow teenage arms make a loop. She has mature, slender legs and a child's torso. Gazelle and hog. Her awkward grace draws attention to the man, by which time his eyes are already on every observer. He seems hungry for any detail his eyes can pick out. It is an attitude Eoin knows well. Two cars from opposite directions pass and the odd pair hurry across to a free picnic bench near the entrance of the pub. The man leaves the girl seated with the car keys and goes inside. Eoin follows him.

Men, regulars, are seated at the right-angled bar. At least they are regular enough to allow loud imprecations pepper their talk. Whatever they are talking about interests all of them: they each vie to quip, though one of them appears to be dressing the conversation most to his own taste. Differences in their age and appearance, as well as a lack of partiality to any one from another, a certain intra-communal alienation, imply that these men have arrived at the pub separately. No seven men (there were no women present except for the elderly bar woman with bark-like skin who comes and goes through a door behind the bar, and a student) in a rural pub could have differed more. Perhaps each represented a constituency. One of them, the one speaking the most, is about forty. He seems to be a farmer. A sparse beard covers his neck and jaw line; the rest of the face is almost hairless. He is not so much fat as inflated. His round jumpered body has a pressurized drum-like quality, not really a human shape at all. He must have sheared a lot of sheep, or cocked a great deal of hay that day because he looks prepared to face anything, even death, such is his air of satisfaction with his lot. He is a man to be envied, perhaps. He drinks, smokes and speaks freely and with the clearest conscience.

The voices of the men drown out the sound from a TV behind the bar until the Mercedes driver speaks. He orders two cokes and two bags of crisps. He says 'crasps'. The locals, too at home to ignore him, regard him with friendly fear and it falls, as if by birthright, to the bulbous farmer to account for their sudden break in talk, with a remark of introduction.

'Down for a week's holiday,' the northerner replies, 'mighty weather down here.'

'Oh yes, we are blessed altogether this summer,' says an old man wearing a well-worn suit.

'Ah sure, I love it down here,' says the visitor, agreeable, quickly locating the most recent speaker. And then one by one the other men take turns to add a pleasantry and the northerner replies to each one carefully; all except for the farmer who has become conspicuously quiet. He appears to be taking offense. The glow of satisfaction moments earlier has turned to pre-occupation. Hostility burns in his eyes. But it is difficult to say why. The news comes on and he begins to take a sudden interest in the TV, straining to catch the words. As he listens, the sound of the northerner's voice, deep and hollow, competes with the newscaster and the farmer's lips tighten. He glances repeatedly at the northerner who each time anticipates him but without apparent concern. The rest of the men ignore the farmer. They are too interested in this northerner.

Eoin, beside the student who is standing by the entrance waiting, finds himself taking to her. He does not want to order anything yet. Near the girl he realizes he has developed a feeling of pity for her, for being in this pub. A spontaneous feeling of protectiveness emerges, though he barely noticed this girl earlier. She is leaning on one leg; her thin arms dangle or else move self-consciously. She has the shy emptiness and daring of one who forces themselves into a situation their instinct tells them to avoid, trusting that some part (maybe all of it, who knows?) of their experience will be worth something later; determined to face life, at least for now, indiscriminately and without prejudice.

She comes from Dijon. She loves the countryside and nature. Her favorite animal is the barn owl. They nest in her grandfather's shed every year. She used to listen to the hooting every night and misses it. Sometimes she would see one flight (she means flying) on bright nights from her bedroom window. Her breath has a dairy smell, like evaporating milk, and the more Eoin smells it the more he forgets where he is, the more he worries when he remembers again. The more he hears about Dijon and France, the more he sees her as trapped in the wrong place.

She is twenty, a similar age to Eoin. Her birthday was last Sunday. She tells him she studies sociology. She says she is unique but thinks her father wanted a son instead, and he receives that remark carefully. He gives the corresponding facts of his life. He is a mechanic he tells her because, he patronizingly thinks, it will be easy for her to understand, and anyway it is not entirely untrue. Claire is her name, but she has to repeat it for him because he is expecting something more French. He has to repeat Eoin, and spell it twice. They both must be deaf! When she says certain words, and when she smiles, something occurs at the edges of her upper lip revealing an inner fold that Eoin has never seen in a human's lips before. It gives her mouth an expressive articulation that makes up for her faulty English. Her fingernails are small and unpainted, the cuticles look like they would break easily. She uses her delicate hands for emphasis and also simply for style. But it is her lime-green eyes that upset him the most. They fix on his with a trust that encourages him to speak on. The desire to talk more and the effort to overcome it sharpens his senses and sobers him, that and the northern man whom he has not forgotten about while speaking to Claire.

The man from the North is in no hurry to return to the table outside. He sips his coke and goes on talking and listening and observing. Through gaps in the concentration he devotes to Claire, Eoin hears them talking about football. The sports round up at the end of the news has ended.

'Was he going for him at all, I wonder,' the northerner says.

'Oh he was of course,' says the old man in the suit.

'He tried to break him up.' This from a young man with smooth hair who has not said much up to now, and seems to have worked up a great effort to speak, which the northerner rewards with a generous look his way.

'I think myself he pulled out at the last minute,' says a prosperous looking man who had been playing golf earlier. His cupped scorecard is on the bar cradling a little pencil.

'Aye,' says the northerner in conclusion, addressing all of them it seems, though looking at the farmer, 'You think so?'

Each one utters something different, in concert, before going abruptly quiet, perhaps to think some more about whom his question had been intended for. The farmer looks from the northerner to the other men and then all around the bar. There is no sign of the old woman.

'Hey,' he roars, and makes a second show of searching the room for service.

Everybody turns to look at the French girl except the northerner who continues to watch the farmer, and Eoin who watches the northerner.

'Yes,' she jumps up from the wall bench where she has just sat down facing Eoin, and goes quickly to fetch the woman, full of urgency.

'A moment please.'

As she passes through the bar the farmer says loudly: 'pint of stout.' Thinking it is right to do so she hurries onwards to the door leading to the private quarters where the woman and she cohabitate. But not replying to the farmer turns out to be wrong.

'Hey!' This time she freezes with her hand on the handle of the open door. All on her own, she looks back at him.

'A minute please, my arse. A pint, please, right this fucking minute, please.' His voice turns soft but his eyes are flint.

'I'm sorry, sir, but I have not the permission to pool the pint.' When she says 'pool' Eoin's heart plunges for her having to deal in words that have no significance for her, but are part of the swill that is exchanged among the swine who gather at this insignificant trough night after night. Words that are badges of her mistake or, shall we say, misjudgment.

'I will get Mizus Flavin. It won't take a moment.'

'Didn't you hear me…?' The raised voice has shed its softness, ironic or otherwise, and a chuckle comes from one of the other men, perhaps an attempt to loosen the tension. But not receiving an authenticating echo, it makes matters worse. The northerner wears a relaxed expression that, given the atmosphere, is a smirk. He looks amused. In comparison the other men look ashamed though not yet angry. All except the golfer who seems to be eagerly anticipating a variety of potential developments.

'One is not permitted to oppose a father,' a voice inside Eoin's head reminds him. 'But one is free to challenge all others.' He consults his understanding. 'There are enough others.'

'…or are you deaf?' says the farmer, softly again, with another smile.

The deaf word up again, but now from a violator. A palimpsest of feelings produced by the same word in the same foreign language that this girl has elected to learn with romantic hopes. The farmer's shit-flecked boot now sits prominently amid the clean association between Eoin and the student. That is what Eoin imagines. He imagines that this woolly-headed man also stands between her and Ireland. That he has pricked a huge delicate bubble. Now she would have to blow a new one, smaller, less iridescent, and look out for this type of prick in the future. That is what Eoin imagines, as he looks at the northerner who is unperturbed, as though the scene were precisely what one might expect in a place like this, or perhaps anywhere, and for that reason, that familiarity, it is as reassuring as the taste of salt. It is what he has come for. That is what he projects at least. It is the same look worn by the farmer before the northerner turned up. Who knows what mysterious forces turn tables.

In a daze the girl releases the handle and moves away from the door toward the beer taps. The farmer makes a sign of approval by putting a cigarette in his mouth, releasing her from his glare, and flicks a glance at the northerner before setting it alight. But he is too late. By now the newcomer has a coke in each hand and a corner of both crisp bags between his teeth. He glances at Eoin as he passes through the doorway but he stays seated until the old woman appears through the door that has been left ajar, all a-bustle, and the girl makes her frightened flight through that same private gateway. On the farmer's face is a new look. It is a look of shame that is pitiful to behold.

Eoin at last comes outside with two bottles and finds Aaron sharing the northerner's table and crisps.

'Harry Hou-fucking-dini, eh?' says Gerry then sips his coke. 'Quite the escape artist. Been looking all over for you. You've got to keep in touch from now on, you hear. Just been telling wee Aaron that.'

The young girl gives Eoin a jailer's stare. The implacable devotee. It is a stare that Gerry hires if he is too distracted by other business.

'I've a wee bit a news, so I have.'

TEN

Suffocating, I awake gasping and recall my dream. I am with Eoin. I am walking beside him with my arm around his shoulder, talking to him. He is looking up at me eagerly but he cannot understand my words. He repeats some of them back to me, as if to show that he is really trying to follow what I'm saying. But what he repeats is gibberish, different from what I have said. There are others around us listening and watching. I am aware of this, it makes me self-conscious but not Eoin, it appears. He is abandoned to the effort of comprehending and communicating with me. I begin to notice that he is reluctant to say something off his own steam, as though he judges my words are more important than his own, and must not be interrupted however incomprehensible they are. He is patient and interested, attempting again to understand my strange words by repetition. The others are beginning to laugh at us, at our apparent failure to relate. Eoin does not take any notice. For his sake I act as though I too do not notice them. For some reason my bad knee is throbbing more than usual, like it received a fresh blow or has become infected. I am limping because of it. The sensation sets my mind to enquire what caused the pain but there is only the vapor of a memory that vanishes the closer I draw to it, returning vaguely when I try to turn my attention away and back to Eoin.

I do not mention this to Eoin of course. It is enough trouble trying to make him understand the basic things I need to tell him. By now the others, as if they could read my mind, are leaping into the air and then squatting down, slapping cupped hands against their healthy knees, grinning with enjoyment that I believe is spiteful. Eoin pays no heed to them. Then I see where we are going: to the bank to withdraw money. I need money to give to Eoin and to pay for the things we need to buy, during the remainder of that day at least. I offer my card to the machine but it will not fit the slot, it is too wide. I search for another but there are no more. It makes no sense. But there is nobody to hear my protest. I have to face that there is no money. But Eoin does not understand this, or perhaps thinks it is unimportant. He waits patiently and contentedly for me to do whatever it is I decide to do next. I realize we cannot go on without money. But I cannot explain that to him and even if I could, what good would it do? I would still need to find money to continue to be with him and to continue talking.

The other people are gathering closer to us, watching my frustration grow and sensing, as animals sense, that what they perceive is only the tip of an iceberg I keep submerged because they know I must hide it from Eoin. It gives them great pleasure to finally have what they have waited years for: proof of the person I really am. And they believe there is more proof to come. They are waiting for the moment when Eoin will see all that they can see. That will be their climax.

It is so dark, and so late. I have no idea what to do. I cannot decide how to proceed. Eoin looks so honest and non-expectant. He will go along with anything, it seems. I have only to lead the way. I try to forget the money and the plans I had before this problem with the card. I almost succeed. I come very near to being free of my old concerns, accepting the simple joy of what I have despite everything: my connection with Eoin.

Just then some rocks land beside us and I hear a cackle of cowardly, familiar laughter, and that is the moment I forget about Eoin and his innocence, and turn my complete attention on those enemies.

Surging anger brings magnificent relief from my torment and the throbbing in my knee vanishes. I smile like some god. Then I run like a god. With one of their rocks, the largest one, held in my hand I kill swiftly and effortlessly, and I begin, instantly, to fall in love with the cries that issue from each skull that, when cracked, reminds me of a popping pea pod. And there is another, almost silent sound. The blooming of fragrant flowers. My revenge plays like a lament from a flute inside my own head. Nobody else can conceive of this kind of courage, or mercy, as I deliver each lethal blow. They run. But what for? On their springy little knees they run, but I catch up with them. Sometimes I strike on the back of a head without breaking my stride, and while they totter and drop I descend upon the next black-blooded arachnid and I make sure to bellow an instant before I swing the death-blow because I want to hear the whimper originate in health, and to see the shoulders hunch and the brace for what they expect to come and cannot escape. I do not disappoint a single one of them. Who is next? Crash! Who next? Crash! Too late to live but you can plead for mercy, for a mercifully swift end.

I am covered in splashes of blood and the smell of buttery iron is exhilarating. It is the only texture that can balm my scorching soul. Around me it mats hair, dying all colors to black. I must finish them all and, do not worry, I do. When the last of the vermin is skull-punched and stilled I win a pure and quiet peace.

There is but me remaining, on the open plain and the cleansing air belongs to me. The corpses are mine too, though I have no more use for them now that they are each arranged and wearing expressions that are much more to my liking than before. It is safe for my hope to come out again. I had hope, I am nearly certain of that. Yes it will come out again, I am nearly certain of that too. Once I find out where I am. I have come a long way during the slaughter. I will go back to where I had been before, and then I will remember my hope. It was something I wanted to say, to somebody. It will come back to me soon if I can remember where I had been before.

Dawn now and everything looks different. Hard to say from which direction I came. I can see nothing familiar for miles in any direction. I will wait for the sun to rise. Then I will see more. Then I will decide what I had wanted to say and do before I forgot. Meanwhile I will enjoy this new dawn, curiously original, incomprehensibly dramatic when I can ignore my throbbing leg that pulls my attention away. I start to hear voices carried on the warm breeze. Strange, foreign voices that laugh and plot yet there is no one living but me. Where are the owners hiding that I cannot find them on this vast flat treeless plain? I move about heavily, my knee aching once again, leg dragging. But there is only the voices.

Then I remember that I left someone waiting, someplace, for me. Sudden panic frees a nagging memory that will not be still long enough to examine. An urgent impulse to act in the name of duty, a repeatedly-roared command whose beginning is incoherent. I flinch with obedience to blindly begin this thing I must do. My knee immediately protests and I am reminded of my limitations. Where is he? What were we going to do? What did I promise? What did he ask for? Each step is a painful futility but I cannot assuage the deafening imperative any other way. I lurch in the direction of the low hanging sun because it blinds me, reminds me of something eternal and pain-free just beyond my world. Its type of relentless and resigned movement, and the quiet company it offers, dignifies my loneliness as well as my dry throat.

'You are crying, Papa.'

And so I am, the last wringing while half-conscious, clutching to the receding reality I now recognize, through My, as dreamwork. By my side, one hand smoothens the deep lines on my face that she seems to think is unsightly about me. Awake, I still have to come to terms with my limitations, how far I am from Eoin. I might have found him again, bad knee or no, if I had not been awakened, or I might have died trying, hauling myself round an arc of parched plain toward the sun. And if I had failed to find him? A worthy death my expiation.

Outside, the worker's voices have acquired a new significance. They had been lurking unseen among the magenta hills fringing the desolate plain, besmirchers of the peace that followed the annihilation. It was they that brought me to tears (tears of frustration, note, not sorrow) that everywhere I attract enemies, whether with Eoin, or away from him. Enemies are limitless. No matter how many I slaughter or maim to benignity, there are more, somewhere else. The peace I know is transitory, only I am stationary. And Eoin is gone again.

I get up from the bed, sit on the red chair feeling worthlessly wise again as a young boy in a strange house, of strange smells and troubled people, wrapped in the marmoreal casing of old man's flesh. I have nothing to say. That is the proudest fact of how I feel. Apropos of no matter can I think of one apt word. My mouth has become a sarcophagus, my tongue a mummy. And my eyes, treacherous torturers, are introducing me to the extraneous I have no stomach for. I want to close them. How similar am I to Eoin? What whim or wind has put me here in this place, now? Of what larger plan was I (am I still?) an unwitting part? How much do I still not know after all those years of asking? Or is the knowledge I seek all contained in a single small chest? All or nothing? Hit or miss?

Of course I know nothing after a near-lifetime! I have not found the treasure yet. But I have some knowledge, if only of narrow value. The treasure is not in any of the places I have so far looked. That is the significance of the nothing that discourages me at each turn. Of course it is nothing! Nothing is nothing as everyone knows. I have not found understanding yet, but each day I am surely closer to it. Yes, I am narrowing my search (but by how much, or how little?) Eventually I will find it, or else I will die searching, and that will be fine, because death will be an interruption, not an ending. I would not have given up. I will not have presumed my failure. I will not have forsaken Eoin. I will not have been augured.

ELEVEN

'Speak! Any words will do. The effort will eclipse the meaning, or the lack of. Nobody will care what you say, or they will quickly forget, paraphrase you later in better or worse terms according to your effort, which they will remember better than the words. Good lad, say what comes into your head. It'll be all right in the long run. Any words. Go on, we are listening. You can say anything you like. You have the floor. What have you to be afraid of?'

The voice in Eoin's head is running apace with Gerry's bit of news.

It speaks about an ugly head, similar to a younger Aaron's covered in curls resembling dirty winter wool. But the slanting yellow eyes are the wrinkled and narrowed eyes of an old miser, not a seven year old. A rectangular freckled band spans the center of the flattened face. Below it a puck's nose tip, above it the eyes looking out, one sadistically more closed than the other (if ever a face threatened to haunt!). The expanse of unkempt hair is a paragon of neglect. Every lock continuously reasserts its punkish independence with the help of the mass of maggots multiplying with Cambrian vigor off the scratched scalp and the cleanly torn neck. The face is barely marked. His back had evidently been turned, or there had been gaps among the spray of hot fragments. The electricity box had pinioned most of the shredded body while the hurricane lifted the head away between two buildings where it came to rest gently on a mound of plastic bags, filled with food waste, and sodden cardboard boxes with pictures of fruit.

This rotting woolly head is not found for days after the explosion (the trash collection service is delayed that week). The man credited for its discovery claims to have seen it the first day but, aware of how vulnerable one can be to suggestion following an attack, vowed not to allow the bastards get to him. Later, when he hears they are missing a head, his imagination is by then already loose and running wild. He feels nostalgic, sad, and this has a less than salutary effect upon those who are his friends. It gives him a peculiar comfort to pity the head and, by inference, the person it had belonged to for having had to remain unknown for a time, though only a few days. Nevertheless, and no need to exaggerate, the head means more to this man for having lain a few days in disguise. But it is not in disguise. It is starkly exposed! If only it were charred or looked more like a rubber mask or a punctured football he might have had the courage to examine it sooner. His life is not the same afterwards. He is racked with a mysteriously elusive guilt that, though unable to stand up to his intelligence if confronted directly, clings to him at all other times like a fishy odor, sickening but strangely attractive.

Gradually this man spends more time alone, something that is not intentional in the beginning but, the trend established, he becomes biased to its qualities though recognizing it will eventually lead to extreme isolation. Yet he is unable to make the effort to rehabilitate because it has occurred to him, with frightening clarity, that the past was not better than now, and his imagination has been hijacked by terror. He becomes a fatalist. If he is to be increasingly alone, he thinks, it is because he needs time to understand the guilt, and that can only be done passively. It will come to him, he thinks, the reason for his guilt, and for everybody else's. He dies many years afterwards, alone and confused.

'I don't want to do this anymore,' says Eoin after Gerry has gone.

'What? What else would you be doing? Who'll give you a job when that's gone?' Aaron points to the envelope rolled up in Eoin's fist.

'They have your name. Gerry has your name. You're his soldier. You signed the paper. He has your name. He will find you.' He thinks a moment. 'Like he did today.'

The envelope with one thousand pounds in new red fifties feels like a surveillance device. In its presence it is difficult to talk about escaping.

'Manchester. I'll open a garage with this. I'll work for myself. I'll restore old cars, Volkswagens.'

'What do you know about Manchester?' continues the devil's advocate.

'Coronation street. That's all you need to know. I've seen how a garage runs there. And the people look decent and cheerful. I could get along there.'

Blonde-boy's arms go up and he is lost for suitable words.

'Oh yeah…that's all you need to know? *Carnation* street. Ace.'

'And it's cheap! At least a pint is cheap; and milk and papers. You can judge other things by that.'

'You don't drink pints! Or read papers! How do you know that anyway?'

'Carnation street! I'm telling you. It's only a program but they have to use real prices or else nobody will believe the rest of it.'

'Nobody *does* believe the rest of it.'

'You know what I mean. It's got to be close to reality. Close is close enough for me. It'll do for me. I'll make a start there. They'll never find me. I'm going after this.' He raises the fist of Irish money and brings it down like a gavel.

'I'll see you when you get back.'

'Give over. You're going as well. They'll get you to tell them where I am, otherwise. They'll give you no peace until you do.'

'I won't open my mouth.'

'They know you will, because they think I'll have told you the kinds of things they can do. The police are more fiction than Carnation Street. Gerry's army is the reality. You know that much already. If I didn't tell you where I was going they would kill you before they even considered believing that. But look a minute, would you, what are you leaving behind? A dole check and a sparring partner twice your age?'

'This is my home, my country!'

'Some fucking home!' Eoin stops laughing abruptly. 'You can come back in the future. Anytime. It's not China.' The weight of China! He shouldn't have said that.

'Wait 'til you get there. See all the flange. You won't be pining for long.'

'Coronation street?'

'That's not reliable for flange. They don't use beauties because it's about hardship and they don't want to stir up the wrong emotions. But still, some of the women they use are crackers in real life.'

'How the fuck do you know that?'

'From the newspaper.'

Manchester grows. It is rapidly cultivated by Eoin, in both their imaginations, into a plausible destination. But it is only when the student comes outside and walks over to Eoin that Aaron sees the bigger picture.

The three speak until after the sun has collapsed into the Atlantic, long after the pub has closed and everybody has gone away, and the same sun has begun to reappear out of Siberia, dawn fatigue rubbing them with the sleep they did not get. By then all three of their lives have taken what some would call a turn, a dramatic turn. But it does not feel dramatic at the time.

The dawn is the dawn of a simply arranged world, the final conversion of hope after a prolonged period of waiting, into a spray of fresh, farther-reaching hopes, sprung forth, the vast space captured inside coming into focus as their future, their world in the future.

Aaron goes to the car to sleep first. At the moment the two are alone, Eoin experiences a moment of near perfection. It is a sensation that he is certain could not have been improved or augmented, at least not within his living experience. Every nerve with any potential to deliver pleasure to and from his brain is in action to that end. Every smell locked within the morning moisture is presented in labeled particles; each chattering bird is working for him separately. Claire's face, all of the parts, is attended to by teams of specialists, who reproduce dozens of replicas with subtle variations, and place them with care inside his memory. Each word she speaks is archived with an archaeologists concern. In a few hours he has captured some immense concert of experience that fits neatly into the space created by his doubt. It is a brief, and complete event. Afterwards he will have to strive to be complete again, now that he has glimpsed its worth.

He offers her his kiss and she drapes two thin arms over his shoulders and around his neck. Her eyes shut. Her breasts touch his chest. As he meets her mouth he wonders what he would have done had they not met, how he could have managed to live without this new perspective. The current events appear in dream textures and colors, shades different from any reality he has so far known. Although he does not yet know how, he suspects that he will have to verify this night, or else verify his life up to now. Something would have to yield, to die back, in his estimation of what was real and unreal.

A rootless sense of capability comes to his aid. He is wide awake again, the sun clear of the fields, dawn fatigue past. They have to part now for a while. He, at least, has to leap from the cliff he realizes he has always stood on, and fly. When they part with their promises Eoin wants more than anything to be able to fly.

TWELVE

Whispering voices, as a rule, have always made me uneasy. I often wonder is it the same, finally, for everyone. Voices in French most of all. Perhaps they are not talking about me. But whether they are, or are not, makes no difference. It is purely in the sound, the source of the unease that, to me, is more distressing than a shout, though I care little for shouting voices either. They are second on my list, after whispering voices. It gets worse, let me say, this spiky sensitivity to *sous voix*, as I get older. Maybe it is that because I grow deafer each year more voices reach my ears as whispers. When I hear whispering it is like a finger, its yellow nail overreaching the tip, prodding my bellybutton. How to describe the sensation springing from that? Could it be said to be out of the run of things?

A funny thing is the hypnotic drowsiness. It is part of the problem. The onslaught just when one most needs to be alert. I suspect that is what overcomes those who are said to have died peacefully, in old age. The last pleasant sound falls and is lost to a whisper, and now every moment of one's waking warmth is experienced to a soundtrack of incessant whispering, even pages whisper. The no longer prodding but sustained pressure of that finger against one's bellybutton that makes living too exhausting finally. It is just a theory. But I wish I could know in advance, know for sure whether anybody else shares my notion about old age and whispers.

'He started hearing voices shortly before he died.' How often has that been said to cue automatic head shaking among the not-surprised? But who digs around to examine the killer voices, to find out how long one has been hearing them? I do. I hear Eoin's voice, and I sometimes hear Claire's, and they are close to whispers. The farther away and dimmer they are because of time, the clearer they sound. They are unmistakable. The other thing that is unmistakable is that I welcome them. I am not insane. I know they are long gone, that it is all inside my head. But I do hear them, from the outside through my ears, just as if they were here, speaking to me in almost whispering voices. I must tell you this because I think it is important: the truth is I sometimes look forward to hearing from them. Sometimes I even worry whether, uneasy or not, I could go on with this, with this business of hanging on, if I did not believe I would continue to hear Eoin and Claire speaking to me in whispers.

I am aware of a development. It seems to be beyond my control. I do not dread it, only parts of it. I am coming to a point, it seems. Some days I hope I do not reach it. Other days I crave it. I am glad then, that it remains beyond by control. Otherwise it is almost certain I would usher in the wrong outcome, without realizing it was the right one or, just as likely, vice-versa.

Unlike you, the cocksure man in the bed next to me would not understand. If I mentioned whispers to him it would lead to whispers, in French (he thinks I speak Cambodian well, but not French, because I am clever about what I say), concerning me. But what of the muck he calls ideas, holds dear, in silence? Let us not be unfair to Francois, to apply the name yet another somebody gave to him, or Frank as I think of him because it serves me better, has more bounce, like a plank, and when I find a word like plank I see myself standing on the end of a diving board and springing off Frank's head into an open swimming pool that is very blue. And then I am in France, a place I could never take you, where I had imagined correctly I would long for, for so long.

But it is worse without whispers, I must admit. There are days when they are absent, or parts of days which, if they fall around the time I awake, are the worst. It appears, then, that my shattered knee has me all to itself. At those times I must sit and approve its monstrously monotonous cabaret, hidden from sight, through the vibrations it sends through the medium of simple, physical pain. The scarcer the whispers, the better the performance (the sharper the pain), I suppose it thinks, and I tend to agree because it is the only yardstick I have.

My knee and I have a conflict of interest. I still own most of it but detest it and do my best to ignore it. It reviles me and uses any opportunity to win my recognition, however hate-filled it thinks that recognition will be. This knee is quite possibly the purest case of evil-mindedness, something that is never easy to instance, despite what goes around. How clever the knee! Without its cooperation the leg is a prop and the good leg might as well be too. The whole ambulatory apparatus shuts down, and action, worthwhile action, all action that is worth more than its own self, becomes impossible.

Still, I got here. Although I admit I do not understand how. It's as if when I look backwards over a shoulder I see images of the path I took and can not judge whether it had been that way as I was passing through, or if the desert I see happened apace with my movement, always one step behind. Some terrible wrecking device tethered to my waist, moving with me, demolishing new life an instant after encountering me. At other times I see a series of beautiful oil-paintings that arouse such intense nostalgia I cannot abide myself for letting them slip away from me, for not having stayed within one of them, for not allowing myself to be bound in pigment alongside all that I had previously loved, smiling permanently in an everlasting context, for some other living mind to like. Or to love.

It is hard to explain this concern of mine with the past. No, I do not mean the future. I mean the past. Enough gets made of the future.

*   *   *

The mistress. Eoin was important to her. She said many things to him and he came to know her by them. Knowing her, he knew how to behave. He loved her, she succeeded in that regard I need not intimate. After being three months alone with his father, the prospect of going to live with a woman he did not know, who had caned him only once, was not dreadful. But from when he left the house where his father had lain in bed with the bedroom door locked, and drove in the mistress's car to the deserted school on that first day of the Christmas holidays, his worry turned to the day when he would have to meet his father again. It was an absolute pre-occupation. Any possibility for the emergence of good that might lay hidden inside that strange man was, by Eoin's departure, extinguished because it depended on the continuation of Eoin's seven years of faith, now broken. The boy somehow knew but couldn't understood that the greatest significance of this act of desertion lay in the relinquishing of that faith, in its symbolic weight.

From that day of recurring significance, as if to take responsibility and compensate for his acquiescence to the mistress, Eoin tried hard to remember his father purely as the kind and decent man he wanted to be, and no longer as the type he actually was. A portrait became fixed in every corner of his approaching new world—the world he was now guided through by the mistress—of this man. Everything that ought to be real and worth admiring flowed from that portrait and filled up fantasies of his own personality. It did not matter that those ideas had never been and could never be in the life he had known and would come to know through the friction of action. It mattered only that they offered protection against other people's scathing happiness.

All the world was in relation to Rush and the potatoes, gritty crumbs of loam, and close air that amplified the crows. Drying colors, pure and modest covered the fields and they had laughed at his father for his buffoonery.

'A big baby,' she had said of his father and then, 'thank God for my big man.' She meant Eoin and it caused him to squirm under the natural secretion of her beautiful power, her easy solidarity with their surroundings that placed his father, for once, at her mercy. A terrific tranquility stood before him but cut off from him, requiring her mediation.

She made Eoin delirious with wonder at how she could, so effortlessly, be part of all this indefinite perfection; how she had been a hare who risked allowing her leverets to graze some way into the wilderness, to experience the confection of life, to understand that there are things that will never not be there, will never leave you, to show that only you can, and will, leave first, when the time is right. And the promise to come back again another day, to eat steaming potatoes from the van, butter chips subsiding, leaning back on the sacks.

'I ask nothing more than for that,' Eoin would tell himself, and for the promise of a touch that could almost be felt, that was itself a promise, among the three of them, to be kind to each other from now on. All the world at peace.

I can tell you that the mistress liked avocado and disliked banana, even the smell of banana. Eoin would have to get used to such declarations that felt like threats to him as well as his father who loved bananas. In practical matters she now ruled. She showed him how to cover his books in brown paper, ample of the good stuff off a roll from Eason's, not paper bags, not pieces of potato sack. Some evenings she cried. For him. For what he had suffered, she said. It was over now she would conclude each time, and tell Eoin that she understood what his father was like.

Strangely for Eoin, he found it possible to accept what she said. It was not Eoin's fault, he must not blame himself or feel guilty for the way his father was. For the last exhortation the mistress applied distinct force. It was a crowning statement that, placed at the top of a moiety of talk, cast a retrospective veil of sanctity over those earlier words. In fact when she said he must not blame himself or feel guilty or ashamed it reminded him—the feeling that came over him, the resistance that he found himself trying to overcome—of the times when his father would tell him: be your own man. There was the same deliberation over the words, the same certitude, in both of their tones that was weaker or absent at other times. It was an ominous call to overcome something he could not quite make out but accepted on faith for the time being, blaming his age for the glitch. The words, to him, held an infinite, flexible, insubstantial but dogmatic and inescapable truth though, of course, he never said that even to himself. From the serious looks that went with it, Eoin presumed he would discover the meaning in the fullness of time. He need not be overly alarmed at the present moment, he reasoned, simply be aware of the unidentifiable entity coming over the horizon, and remember who had given it a name for him to know it by, perhaps thereby entitling them to a claim on him.

*   *   *

After dinner in a nice house I thought I had forgotten, not in Africa I believe, but sometime before or after (it could have been Japan because it was not France or America I assure you, Ireland either; and not England) I saw a look that horrified me. I shall not forget that look. If it had not found me I dare say I would not be here today. Yes, it was Japan. I remember the place now. It was after dinner and the small plates and chopsticks had been cleared away. My wife's (I had a wife) genial father had his hands clasped loosely on the table where he sat farthest from the pianist, my wife. Interposed, at the opposite end of that table that had other sitters I will not mention, my seat was turned and I sat still with a deliberately masochistic twist in my neck.

From my position at the fringe of the table I could see only my wife among the gathering, to whom I was closest. I had to crane my neck almost equally the other way if I wanted to observe anyone else. Yet they could all watch me, furtively, throughout the performance, though I had not considered that until I saw the expression I wish to mention. How shall I describe it now, without wasting time on the man himself or the rest of his family, for only that look I wish to appear in my story, at least for the present? Ebbing tolerance? It was inscrutable at the time, I believe. It was many things and nothing to me, all fitting once I had made the necessary appraisal of where I was and what grounds, or lack of, I had for being there. In fact, it was the only expression he could have offered me at that point, the point when I lapsed under a reckless fancy of imagined familiarity. Not knowing better, I made the error of assuming that the fraught atmosphere that I was enjoying, or not enjoying—my memory is questionable on that issue, experiencing is better—to be familial. As my wife's small right hand rippled and trilled the newly tuned keys I could not help myself from unwinding my intoxicated head and swiveling it past all who sat in between, to him.

I should have foreseen—and might have too, had I not allowed my famous alertness to lapse—the consequences of my act. To share the love of the woman he had loved first was not what my wordless panorama meant to him.

'See what I have caught in my net?' was closer to his reading of it. 'And with the meanest of effort. Look what I am capable for luring! Consider my ease! Imagine what I could do if I put my heart into it! What far greater beauty and talent I could command!' That, I believe, is what this kind man reacted to when his face turned suddenly, and he dropped his gaze upon his hands, and began worrying his gums. It might have been a broken tooth, or a bitten tongue. But I could not take that chance. I was incapable of taking that chance, now alert again. There was simply more evidence, however ineffable, to the contrary. I have always observed a *balance of probabilities* verdict on life, eschewed the unreachable *beyond reasonable doubt*, which nevertheless I hoped, and still do, I admit, to reach in that future era, the fullness of time.

Over the course of the days that followed, I managed to steady my thoughts by surrounding the incident with a padding of insignificance. For I had no treatment. Now, many years later, I still have no balm, but the gangrenous padding has been removed. I wanted that man to love me. If not then hate would do. That night I was closest to winning his hate at the moment I felt love had its first real chance. How funny. How mistaken. How I had offended that good father with my outrageous expectations.

Up to that day I had been consistent in my thinking: 'I will go along with you, with all of this, though it runs counter to my instincts, because it is better than not going along with anything, and promises more than going along with the other things I have considered. When is the pay off? When will I get to appreciate the value of all this dazed movement urged upon me from outside? When will I be allowed into the world of the normal and the good and the decent and the loving? And the timely laughter? What must I do to qualify for your sponsorship? I have done all you told me to, to the letter. I was loyal, I was honorable, and I loved everybody I was told to love. Is it not merely a question of more time? Yes? A little more time to go before the fullness is reached? What? You will let me know when it is reached? You will not forget, will you? I hate to complain. It is not that I do not trust you but, you know, I have been waiting for such a long time now. At least, to me—if you will pardon my self-centeredness—it seems a long time. I hope it will not take too much longer, that is all. But I know it is a complicated business, many things to arrange, matters to discuss, more tests to perform. You have your hands full. I would not want to be in your shoes, I guess. I do not know how you do it. Thank you. I am sorry for the trouble. I can wait, of course, as long as it takes. I can wait. Here I can wait. It is the best place for me to wait.'

Branded would be a good way of explaining my feelings before that

Japanese man. Recognized and branded. And out of energy. The obvious course of repair was to pretend to be somebody else, somebody branded in the wrong. But whom? Too many to choose from, unlike earlier times. And too little energy now (I was no longer young). What else? Grant him my unqualified shame and convert to a new faith, be augured anew? That seemed to be the best alternative. But it was not. A third one, previously unthinkable, came into existence, first in my mind. It sprouted from someplace beneath the rubble to save me.

*   *   *

Where am I going with this? Whom am I talking about? Please do not seek clarity yet. Do not rush me. The antidote I mentioned before is starting to enter your vital organs now, but it will take more to save you. I will let you know, my relative, my lover, my *familiar*. But right now you could probably not imagine the color of the tide this night. A whiteness like powder shaken upon the sea. There is a full moon hovering guiltily out of sight I know. I will get outside in good time and pretend to be angry for the sake of the moon's pride. It will not be hard, the air in here stinks. Whatever they used in the kitchen wild game fat is all I can think of now and I am damned if I will let that stench bully me back to Africa tonight. All in good time. All in my time.

'Never be angry at them. Say: "It is nothing, nothing, no need for apology". Don't give them an easy way out by letting your short-lived anger serve as their punishment. Let them think about it, worry about you, and never forget what they did to you. Make them suffer. Prolong their suffering.' That was another pearl for Eoin to remember and put into practice one day. Had he access to the term Eoin's father might have said: don't allow them any closure. I will allow the moon closure for being beautiful, interrupting my darkness, sucking the seawater up close to me to tauntingly dump abandoned wavelets at the entrance to my haven-home. Though I owe them nothing, I will keep them company as they expire, each of those wavelets, up to a thousand or so, and let the smoke sting away at my eyes. How do you account for...? Give me a moment and it will become clearer I hope. These strands of extruded toffee, each has a color. I want to stretch each strand until the color disappears and each grey fiber is alike though you cannot deny they had their earlier color. Stretching took it away? How do you account for that? It has not happened yet; each strand still has its color. How *will* you account for that? is the question. I am giving you fair warning, you see? More than I got, though I am not complaining. Remember: it has nothing to do with the greying of colors mixed. That excuse will not work. I guarded against that, you will remember, kept the experiment, this story, pure. My pure, of course. Not absolute pure. I will let you in on a secret now. I am gambling that your pure is less than mine. But just now I realize this underpinning is worthless unless I define my type of pure. Fine categorization will not do, so let us here agree to another attempt later, shall we? For now just keep your mind on the sweet, thinning threads, and the moon-washed water.

THIRTEEN

Tu-ra-lu-ra-lu-ra, tu-ra-lu-ra-li...tu-ra-lu-ra-lu-ra...A mad woman's shite Eoin's father called their kitchen, the bedroom, the general disorderliness of things. Scutter was the impression it evoked for Eoin. A stream of scutter flowing across the floor with mad force, throwing anything that could be moved out of its way, pitching the rest at a crooked angle. The feces he eventually saw were a flush-beating couplet of cocktail sausages, presented to the melody of an occasionally grunted Irish lullaby. The expulsive effort produced a smell resembling lightly crushed leeks. A mad woman's shite? This? Who can tell? But it was definitely a woman's shite, if shite were feces, and these droppings were the shyest looking things he had ever seen, shyer than a hare, shy enough to leave him apologetic for eyeing them. But now that he was eyeing them, he might as well take his time, get a good look at something rare indeed, something not unlike himself.

Barrels of cargo bobbing above a sunken barque, rolling self-centeredly for a difficult balance. Ha ha! Funny little things, not over with just because they had been discharged from their prized vessel but, emancipated, in possession of a plucky new life, trite life, but life all the same. Apropos of Stan Platt: 'He couldn't hurt a fly,' Eoin lied to blonde-boy to calm him. But to blonde-boy's 'I'm less than a fly' he had no response. Was blonde-boy less than a mad woman's shite? Was he, Eoin? They could be equal was his thought. He wished blonde-boy were here to see this; it might solve a problem for both of them, especially for blonde-boy for whom confronting Stan Platt would have only made things worse. Nothing, perhaps, was less than this woman's shite, yet look at it go! Not bad at all!

*   *   *

Pertussic barking from an upstairs child announces, watchdog fashion, a Hibernian caller. It is an old man from the North with chocolaty teeth and a gentle bearing. Would they mind, the man with a kink in his back, asks, having a wee chat inside. Gerry is concerned, has asked him to check in and say hello. Eoin measures the lie. His manner suggests an entirely different context for Eoin's departure from Dun Laoghaire port one month earlier: that it had taken place openly, even reluctantly, bound for a disclosed address.

'How are you settling in Eoin?' He speaks the name with practiced ease. What coded understanding would Eoin be inadvertently acknowledging by giving an answer? Whatever he says, he senses, will make him more vulnerable.

'Grand.'

Eoin manages to smile, telling himself it is for Claire, though it is only a question of time before he can smile no longer. He aims to keep in check other words impatient to get out and betray him. The man has no trouble making himself comfortable at the dining table by the window of the ground floor flat. He is visibly without urgency. He has all day it seems. The man nods very slowly and maintains a benign expression on his face. There is no sign of suspicion in that face but everything else about the man, his familiarity, and his air of purpose is cast with Svengalian omnipotence. He knows Eoin has run away, but that fact is to this man's advantage. He also knows that Eoin has been found, because he has found him, and has seen with his own eyes the found look on Eoin's face. The relaxed manner highlights the pettiness of Eoin's personal affairs, their harmlessness, irrelevance and contingency upon the lives of others. 'Relax with me,' it seems to say. 'I am not going to hurt you. You have yourself all worked up over nothing.'

Eoin has not run away after all. He is not capable of it, not in their eyes, not by their reckoning, which finally counts more than his own. His own has no basis in reality. His private acts are no more potent than dreams, fragmentary and, because dreams are dreamy, without any bite. They do not matter very much to other people.

'This is the wee lass, I suppose.'

'Claire, this is John from Ireland,' is the best he can do but the old man seems perfectly satisfied with it.

'Pleasure to meet you. John Brophy is my name.' He puts emphasis on the surname, like a clansman. 'Glad to see you're taking good care of the wee boy.'

'Wee lass' and then 'wee boy' holds a possessor's tone. Eoin's heart groans. Claire's hand, when it is touched, symbolizes for Eoin a swamping of hope whose enormity has to be denied because it cannot be justified by anything that has occurred in the flat, so suddenly and so gently. In the touch of the long smoked fingers there is a vampire nip.

'I'm in Whalley Range. Number 223. You'll have to come up sometime for a cup of tea and a chat. I'm at home most of the time. Be lovely to have you. I know what it's like to be away from home, you need somebody to check in on you now and again.' He turns specially to Claire. 'I suppose you have a few friends here Claire.'

'I do, of course (she pick up this expression from Eoin). There are quite a lot of French students at the University and we sometimes meet together and take something to drink (she gives a quick smile and glances at Eoin, the man enjoys that). Or go to the cinema together, and of course we have dinner together sometimes as well...'

'I love France. I have good friends in Paris, you know. Living out in

Vincennes. I haven't seen them in donkey's years. I'll have to pay them a visit while I still can. I'm terrible for putting things off.' He is wistful when he looks back at Eoin, showing he wishes to share a pleasant emotion.

'Which part of the city are you from.'

'I'm not from Paris, no, my parents live...'

'Oh!

Eoin's knee, which has been bouncing higher and higher, hits the table, lifting it slightly. The old man's eyes swivel like a chameleon's but otherwise he does not move, just holds his smile.

'My parents are from Dijon.'

'Oh yes. Must me a beautiful place. Now I am aware of the...

As the old man prattles, Eoin is dismayed to find he is beginning to see Claire differently. This newly developing impression has the power to retrospectively modify earlier ideas, blending them and reducing their color into monotonic plainness, emptiness and so-whatness. When Claire begins to guilelessly report Eoin's plans for the garage, Eoin stands up abruptly. He has to move in order to think better, or try to stop his thinking altogether. The old man breaks off politely from Claire to address Eoin and, with irrepressibly sweet charm, enquires after wee Aaron.

*   *   *

The President of the United States of America, John F Kennedy, visits me. He is interested in helping Eoin. We talk outside on the veranda. He has brought along sandwiches for us to eat, but there is nothing to drink, only the sandwiches of salted salmon with fried egg on slices of white bread. We have one each.

'I hear you are having some trouble with John Brophy, governor of the region,' opens Kennedy the straight shooter. How does he know?

'No,' I tell him, 'Eoin is being bothered, not me.' But wait...I begin to rethink when I see the look on Kennedy's face. I am not fully sure. Is it possible I am being bothered too?

'Well,' he continues, making a head movement like a cow, holding the square uncut sandwich in a palsied hand, the layers flapping open and shut, 'I remember my father paying him a hundred dollars every month. He paid others, but John Brophy was the first to get his, my father made sure of that.' Kennedy laughs, ironically I think, adding, 'Brophy hasn't changed in all those years.' He takes a bite of the sandwich.

Kennedy had a father, I reflect. And now look at the father's son! That fact defeats me. My imagination cannot reach to the extent of his greatness. Yet Kennedy's father, great as he was, could not disregard John Brophy, or else judged it unwise to do so. The man had better be appeased, it seemed.

'Two of my friends took their own lives on account of Brophy,' Kennedy goes on, while chewing, his cheeks packed with sandwich. He laughs again. He seems to be laughing off the words to show they carry no threat for him. But there could have been another reason. I laugh too. It is easy to laugh with Kennedy. He allows it, encourages it even. He is not one of those leaders whose emotions needed to be off kilter from yours. He is not a fragile leader, not in private at least.

'Now, would you consider the States?' he says to me next.

I am about to ask if he means Eoin, but I begin to consider that he is offering me a chance to move to the America. Does he really mean me, or Eoin? As he waits for my answer he seems to turn older and greyer before my eyes, like he has never appeared on television, and he moves more slowly with a wilder shaking of his hands. It is hard to know how to answer him. Is he serious? Is he really here now? Is he not dead? Where are we? It is sweltering on the old weather-beaten veranda. Planks of mildewed wood are crumbling at the end grain. I look at slick ochre mud, brown puddles, violently green grasses and, out on the distant plain, solitary coconut palms stooping their decapitated shoulders. The sky is a bulging chaos of split cloud layers. From someplace the sun is piercing through and reflecting blinding light off the wet ground, evolving invisible steam with essences that sting the eyes and lining of the nose, raise the prickle on Celtic skin.

But what about Brophy? Is this the best way to deal with him, flee to America? Is Brophy not there too? Didn't Kennedy say his father bribed Brophy? Did that not mean in America? What is the point of being there then? What is Kennedy up to? Is he wasting my time? What is his interest in me? His use for me? As Kennedy waits for my response I consider the gamut of questions that make up the present. All I need is one certainty and all the rest will fall into a recognizable pattern.

Behind us a door creaks. I need another moment. Kennedy manages, somehow, to draw out some laughter to give me more time. Does he really know what I am considering, as he pretends to? I add that to my list of considerations. The sandwich is making me thirsty. There are watery impressions everywhere I look, but to drink not a drop. My mind switches between my thirst and all the rest. I haven't a leg to stand on. All I can do is wait, in silence, and hope for a breakthrough. The door of the shack stops creaking and a woman appears. She looks like Eoin's mother. A child runs around her legs and across the veranda, and leaps off into a shallow puddle. My knee twinges as I watch him, and I shudder at the thought of doing the same thing myself. The woman steps down to where the child has leapt and stands waiting for her. Together the pair walk away from me and the shack and veranda, out onto the plain.

Kennedy rises on trembling legs. He has run out of patience with me. When he gets to the edge of the veranda he looks from left to right, sweeping the plain. It is then that I notice the saw-toothed jack-o-lantern profile of the back of his head, and inside the hole is black and glistening. He throws me a glance before climbing down onto the orange mud, then walks off after his family without looking back.

FOURTEEN

Two weeks after John Brophy's visit, a Citroën crawls out of a frosty Manchester and climbs into the Pennines. Beyond the road, everywhere is an out of focus, luminous white interrupted with dark stains that introduce a depraved idea of spring. Through the windscreen the air is clear as iced water and each spurious flake of falling snow feels to Eoin like a dropped letter from a lost color, high and hopeless somewhere amid the sinking grey of an upturned ocean. Desolation to outstrip fantasy stretches in undulations to a glowing skyline in all directions. Tilted substrata supporting a tundral fuzz, compact, rugged and abrasive, now buried in soft aloof ice. The power of the scenery is to establish in Eoin a new frontier in his mind's map of the confines his body must operate within. Some perimeter has become moved to a position previously inconceivable and, beyond which, everything is once again inconceivable, but almost certain, he now suspects, to exist. He must submit himself before this deadly new environment, and die, or else it will kill him; there are places where nothing that resembles him can survive and he has found one of them. Anyway I will die, he tells himself. At least, let it happen in an interesting manner. Let me resign myself to it and conserve energy. Allow all of my fear for all that I see to devour me until nothing is left but myself: a stationary ticking clock, a waiter, an agent, an observation post, a reference. As much dead as alive.

Brophy talks to Eoin as the drives. The radio is on but the volume is too low to recognize the sounds coming out. There is only the presence of sounds. He tells Eoin his mother was a great woman, though she had her failings, like the rest of us. He goes on in a round about of sayings. Eoin misses the key words that the constant theme hangs upon, if there even is one at all. He hears things like 'couldn't hold a candle to her' but misses who or what could not. He never asks for clarification since everything that is said to him seems to be on the pretext of clarification of something else, though lacking, to Eoin, any clarity. They do not matter, those candles, or whatever words Brophy curls his tongue around and issues through the spaced-out stumps of decay in his mouth.

Yellowish oil-slicked locks of hair give Brophy the look of a poisoned seabird whose days are numbered. One who is beyond saving. You can imagine, perhaps, the face. But the most immediate effect of Brophy, and not without the usefulness that smelling salts sell for, is his breath. The air inside the car comes from the church crypt, ancient and rich with slow dry rot and incense striking ever more intense heights of saturation as it wafts over the senses. The mind struggles against what the nose repeatedly warns: evacuate, meantime breathe through a cloth.

Eoin tries to understand. A man so near to death should have other things to do. Eoin is young, it is perhaps excusable in his case. Later he will want to be . . . what is it? Unemployed? Deprived of the relief that work brings? Was it possible he could still be doing this work whether he liked to or not because he would tell himself he liked it; liked it more than any of the imaginable alternatives, because it held that blend of shapes and colors and smells that he recognized himself among. Maybe he could understand a little of the dying seabird. It is as though the poison that is killing him is in the air, or in the food he eats. But if he stops eating it he will die, even sooner, from starvation. Eating poison he remains diminishingly healthy, even happy, until it kills him, gently, he hopes.

Brophy is in good spirits as they drive the polar way. He loves the snow, he confesses, and the memories of making tea from it when they were up against it in the 20's or 30's or '50s. Eoin misses the decade or maybe Brophy contradicts himself. He says 'up against it' like Gerry used to. Was that deliberate? Is Eoin up against it now? Has he already been up against it? Would he be really up against it in the fullness of time? Brophy's growing pleasure is like that of an escapee, groundless glee for a theoretical future. It moves Eoin at times with its scandalous irresponsibility toward what he imagined adulthood should espouse, let alone old age. It seems to call into question what right he himself has to be serious about anything, being still so young. Everyday is a gift, Eoin thinks he is supposed to believe.

He cannot have made tea from snow more than a couple of times, Eoin realizes. It is not Russia. But even once is enough to allow talk about it years later, to trigger warm feelings and laughter. Would he have laughed had he been passing through the snow alone? What does that matter; the old man is stinking to high heavens, and that still trumps all. Yet he is acting naturally enough, as far as Eoin can see, and he knows what he is doing. He knows something beyond what he is doing, that Eoin does not know and tries to tell himself he does not care about, though he does care. It plays with his mind's power switch, stalls him as Leeds grows nearer.

The ginger-haired wirer they meet at the Corn Exchange is called Devlin, Savage Devlin. Devlin thinks his name is a good name, that it was earned by his hair, or for his flair with explosives and electricity. Savage is a hippie, a purveyor of hashish, incense and LSD. He is short and fat and, just before he moves his stubby frame, he gives himself away by a moment of preparation that is foreshadowed in his face. Perhaps he is doing an inventory of his body parts. His movement, when it comes, entails excessive use of the arms and there is a sound, not always traceable, of friction. Savage lives in constant fear of being let down by his body, Eoin thinks, and of it leading to his death. Each call to action reminds him of his precariousness, to which he responds emphatically. He is twenty-four. He makes a three, Eoin reminds himself, after they have finished their fry and Savage brings up wiring—bad wiring.

Savage is a whiz kid. His fingers are better than Gerry's but he evidently does not have the arms and regarding the rest of his corpus, I need say no more. But he has this one glowing skill, extractable from the dross. What he cannot do, or in his queer mind, hopes one day to be able to do, is entirely his own affair. It is not capital today.

'Had to get this wee lad out of the country, after Gerry and all, so we did,' says Brophy, shamelessly folksy, remembering through his tongue that he once had more teeth. 'Somebody saw him, made a connection to Gerry.'

'I suppose it's all died down again by now,' says Devlin, conspicuously, Eoin feels, ignoring Brophy's reference to him. He and Brophy speak as though Eoin is waiting behind a curtain.

'Aye, I suppose a bit aye. But sure you can never tell, so you can't. We're going to keep Eoin a wee bit longer on this side.' Eoin is amused by the ease with which the talk comes.

'I tried to get over for Gerry. Fucking raging.'

'Not at all. Sure he'd a good sending off. Your mother and all was there. The coffin had to be closed of course.' Brophy hesitates before saying more, as though considering Savage's feelings. 'You heard about the head, you did?'

'Poor bastard.'

'Found it in somebody's back garden. Three days after.'

Devlin finally looks at Eoin.

'The rest of him was in tatters.'

Devlin stays looking at Eoin.

'The only mistake he ever made. The solder must have broke,' says Devlin. It sounds rehearsed to Eoin. 'I know Gerry used PearlBond. It goes fucking off too quickly. I bet he was trying to save a few bob.'

Eoin laughs at the last remark. He cannot prevent it.

'What happened to you?' says Devlin to Eoin. 'I thought you were beside him.'

'You've the best part of an egg on your jowls, fat boy. What happened to you? I thought there were none left on the blanket.'

It is Brophy's turn to laugh, as Eoin knew he must, while Savage broadcasts the signal to all around him that he is preparing for action.

'Go easy, he's kidding,' says Brophy, making it two against one that is, as Eoin understands, in his favor. Now he, more than Savage, can say what he wants.

'Gerry went back, said he forgot something. Then bang,' says Eoin flatly, the only one with firsthand information—another important detail. The only one in the world, in fact, with firsthand information of Gerry's demise.

They had found him in the space of a month, Eoin recapitulates inside his head. He suspects Brophy inherited him from Gerry immediately, and then took his time. That Brophy has chosen for the first time to reveal his knowledge of Gerry's death only now, in front of Devlin, is calculated to stun Eoin and expose him to the threat of Gerry's younger brother. And then to protect him, all in one dense scene. Eoin was supposed to become submissive before a godlike intelligence, become pliant again, as he had been with Gerry, and re-attach his loyalty to the organization, accept his inferior place, and be grateful for small mercies: for being allowed to keep his life. But then again, that could all be fantasy. He might be free to walk away, if he chose to, to live in peace, apart from occasional visits from a decrepit man who he could easily send packing, if he chose to. Where was the proof of anything? It is all in his own mind, and not always all there. Whatever way he wanted to look at this situation, he could have it so, could he not? He could kill Brophy with a hard push, Devlin with only a little more trouble. Neither of them regularly carried a gun; a knife would be too embarrassing, even for them. Why was he sitting in a greasy spoon in Leeds with these people he had no time for? The question orbits just beyond his practical thoughts. Why has he left Claire, Aaron and his new planned life, so willingly, to be here?

'You mean you were already away? Are you having me fucking on, wee man?' says Devlin.

Eoin could not have helped himself from laughing even if he wanted to. And he certainly did not want to.

*   *   *

How many perfect days does it take to make a happy life? How many perfect moments a perfect day? I had one moment yesterday. I am quite sure. And one the day before that too. Both were perfect, but swift. My hovers around me like a capable damselfly, landing by my side, brushing my back or the side of my head with a lacy wing and her close body makes a soothing vibration. Touch is her pre-eminent quality. Through it she controls the world within her reach. It is through My's touch that I sense the world. I know nobody like her. She is divine. Solid divinity.

'Can we take a bath?' I ask her again. I do not tell her I want to touch her cunt and her tits with the tips and the backs of my fingers. Instead I tell her it is the only way for me to feel her inner thighs against the only sensitive skin I have left: along the sides of my waist. She has learned to say 'next time'. It has Frank's mark stamped all over it. It is for when, I believe, she would like to say yes, but had better say no. The Cambodian custom of demureness drives me round the bend. There is an equivalent in Khmer but the meaning is bound to be nuanced.

'Next time,' I parrot and when I do she almost laughs and moves to explore my knee with soft pressing fingers that are full of latent hardness. Along the outer rim of the kneecap (she presses my knee down to straighten it) she finds a pernicious knob of bone or cartilage, and begins to describe circles as if to dizzy it into painlessness. And it works. After her fingers have moved on to another zone of my damaged joint, the lingering sensation goes on autonomously. The knob is left feeling like a little prince; the rest of my knee, body and brain his subjects. Of that I am as certain as anything.

'You will feel good, Papa,' she then says to me and I do not presume to know what she means.

'About what?'

'Your story.'

Now she has spoken clearly. I believe her word. Why would she have said this but to spread her wisdom, fertilize feeble life. I had only my usual doubts up till then, but afterwards there are no doubts for hours, even for a while the following day.

'I will feel good at some point in the future, if I keep going and finish it,' I say to myself without mockery; overwhelmingly good perhaps, terminally good. That is my grand goal, and you cannot imagine how tearfully thankful I am during the murmuring night that soon follows for the proximity of her words, when I awake and cannot distinguish myself from my father but for their presence. They are all that keep me still and continuing in the face of eloquent reasoning on the grounds for self-annihilation.

*   *   *

'There are those,' one strand of reasoning runs, 'who will one day ask you to sit down and listen. True spies whose career it is to know more about your life's ending than you will ever be capable of. They will work for a Royal Infirmary or a National Institute of Health, or a Phsar Ream Warmhouse. And they will have other files besides yours.

'That spy (they will most likely be a stranger to you) might have had different news for me,' you will not be able to escape from thinking, 'in which case my ending could have been different.'

'I feel cheated,' you will say. 'How unlucky.'

To be killed by a spy, to have your death post-dated by their words, and to have your imagination pitched into your life's afterward (there has to be a future, right to the end, even if you are not to be any part of it, to balance the past and present of thought against the insanity of time) by another, strange, person. Whatever you imagine it as, it will not feature you. But the stranger will survive you to oversee the wiping up of the last of your mess, and to spy on others. You will love the stranger for their closeness to you, for the guarantee the stranger's career places on witnessing your tangential departure, or for whatever reasons you can find, but above all you will love the stranger for their unconditional ministry. Like a father or a mother; just as important, and therefore just as love worthy. So your thoughts run at one a.m. or whenever you attempt to sleep, in Cambodia, while trying to understand what system requires you, toward the end, to lie and listen to strangers breathing over the sounds of tropical water-lapping.

'How,' goes those thoughts, 'can you die with that shame?' There is no answer. No answer yet. But My says it will come. And I love My more than anyone. I believe in her wisdom. She is patient. She has no choice but to be. I know how that feels. Trust me, I tell her inside my mind, I love you. I love all things. Except ones with fathers. I love the mauled apples. The blighted potatoes. Trust me, you have come to the correct place.

'What are you like?' How many of those who knew me would ask, if they were alive now, and saw me here, as this?

'As what?' I even imagine some voices asking.

'I nearly know,' I would answer to a dog, 'A bit more time and I will be like something decent. Unfinished just now, you see, a terrible state to find yourself in, at any age.'

'But you said you were nearly there a long time ago (a typical dog!),' they ask.   'This time I mean it!' I say (you see, some anger now).

'But…' they query me again, and on it goes, the time-wasting that is talking to dogs. My would never ask me what I am like. She knows what

I am like and it is more, to her, than a pair of buoyant turds. My gains me time. She is comfortable with uncertainty, a yes woman, can-do, can survive outside her comfort zone, risk-tolerant (maybe you are getting a better idea how I made the nest egg that allows me to be here). If these terms mean something to you I am willing to let them stand, as a warm up exercise in manipulation, to show what might be possible for me (I am bristling still from the 'What are you like?' question earlier). If not then I am delighted as well as sorry. I regret bringing it up now, to be honest. But you never know who else will be reading this and I cannot afford to be presumptuous in my unfinished condition, you understand. I have to consider everyone, and not occasionally the ones short of time and patience: especially those ones, my disciplinarians, My's counterpart. Their existence keeps me from straying off into Africa for long periods where I would shatter their sympathy in no time.

But I do not know. I may yet find a way to slip more in because, dear friend, sometimes I am almost certain it is important.

FIFTEEN

The rat-tat of approaching footsteps is a plague foreign to the Cambodia I have known thus far. It does not take a genius to work out why. There is no piece of road smooth or solid enough, no shoes leather enough for the percussive contact. Not in the parts I know. I can only write about what I know, though of what I know I am never fully certain. A weakness? My arse. A curse more like, when you have the ambition I am saddled with to scare people out of their wits.

Up and down I go on tired days looking for a good lie to tell you. To save time, you see. That is all. I have not much remaining. When I remember how little, the prospect of the lie is alluring, to scare you properly, quickly, and be done with it. Then we can move on to other business. The dying. But I do not have the heart. I must persevere with real scaring and it takes so long, for me, using words. I am stuck with this embroidery of what, in the end, is pretty facts, developing not at all as I had intended. And, I worry, not taking me any closer to wiping your mind clean of familiar associations, to filling your childhood schoolbag with chicken heads covered in raspberry syrup, feathers of sugar icing, a cashew beak and gummy bear coxcomb, but real, real vitreous eyes! It does not work like that, does it? It sounds funny to me too, gets me laughing. Like fish oil, boiled black as coffee to boost the health. Truth is, the scaring I crave is likely to be best served by a clean lie. But how can I be certain?

*   *   *

Turkey was too dry for the mistress. She preferred duck but there was none to be had, or goose, so they had a humble chicken for Christmas dinner, Eoin and she, wishbone and all (nothing pretentious in that department). He wondered if she had considered swan, and if not, why not? No clear answer presented itself to Eoin. Too fishy, too beautiful, too lonely to kill? It would put up too elegant a resistance, make one worry if it were not a subversive beneficiary of the Christmas dinner it was scarificed for. Too much waste, perhaps, unless one ate the yellower neck. And who wants a neck, except a Frenchman who has lost a few fingers in the Algerian campaign that would not re-grow no matter how long he lived, no matter how much boiled fish oil he drank, no matter how great his desire to play a nocturne, any nocturne, again? Fingers that could not be coaxed to re-grow except, perhaps, by a helping of well-basted swanneck?

But they were only fingers. At least he could still get a thumb around the trigger guard though it aggravated the frozen shoulder that had also come about with the jolt of defingering and, god love the ducks, they had no idea why he was so mad at them. They looked guilty as can be, flying past, after spotting him with the painfully high elbow, alone, without his daughter for camouflage. Unlucky ducks. No less beautiful for the misfortune of flying into a monomaniac's field of fire. But let us quickly steer away from guesswork. He was perfectly able to clasp the stem of a glass with thumb and forefinger knuckle, or a clay tile from among a pile of rubble. He might well have been able to fling a Frisbee, now that I think of it, had it been an option then. It might have cheered him; so few options back then for rehabilitation compared with now.

That is not guesswork. Not mine at least, but rather the mistress's dinner talk. Blame Eoin, ultimately, for distortions, reductions, amplifications or any light-bending effects. To the equivalent modulations, sound must be susceptible, but I cannot bear to dwell on that thought right at this moment. Maybe later, when I am sure that my story will not fall apart, on account of some detail I have prejudicially ignored that turns out to be a fatal flaw in my whole case against, or for, the past. I am not sure which it will be yet. Either case will do me, a pragmatist at the end of the day, results-oriented, if you care for one last dash of money talk. Consider it a sorbet, if it eases your renewed distaste, a reality check—sorry, that will be the last.

The trifle was gorgeous, and it made Eoin consider the baths they shared in a deeper, historical sense, and look forward to the next one, from where, no doubt, he would reflect upon the trifle in a yet deeper, greater historical sense. That he made a conscious link between the trifle and the bath intrigued him. Oh it was not all abstract, be actually felt the rip of heat along the ridge behind his balls when the cool raspberry sponge parted and the warmer chocolate-sprinkled cream hit his tongue like an over-soft cushion. It was real all right; real and fantasy at the same time. You know what I mean? A usual experience but one that gets argued over by halfwits. But it nearly overwhelmed Eoin for its lack of precedence, and for his belief that it would happen again, like all things did to the very young once the first-time barrier of awareness was breached.

He had prepared slides, the mistress's father, of his Algerian experience, she told him. The land of Aladdin ('more or less', she confessed when he questioned her) with gold, orange skies, yellow sands but most of all blue, blue water with crispy white edges.

'Yes? Yes? Ha ha! Of course I'll show them to you,' and off she hurried, *shiff-shiff* of friction, to fetch the firwood slide box and the projector case of stitched burgundy cowhide; items belonging to another world, a world equally if not more interesting than the Algeria they tried to deflect Eoin's attention toward. The smell of the projector gear mildly etherized him. Ecstasy, slavishness, stupefaction, death even, shock, tears, laughter (a bit of anger too, violent anger); sensual intoxication, as many selfish vying sensations as keys on the piano before his first ever glimpse of Africa, that he could have mistaken for her first too.

'My father had a terrible temper,' she had started to say, more and more frequently, at the beginning of her stories, boring him eventually, until she said it without the laugh, and the idea of progression toward something, and not just passing the time, took hold of him (I cannot say that it was clearer than that to Eoin) and held his interest. How much of her permutated, how much remained fixed was already taking shape in his head.

She would, over time, go on to describe some of the things she remembered her father had done in a temper.

SIXTEEN

The high winter sky, hardened with marble clouds will not settle in my memory for interruptions. I call my memory democratic since my arrival in Cambodia. I believe other people's memories are selective. Both have their faults. If I do not get the weather straight, I am nervous, as a rule. Maybe I have the wrong day, I begin supposing, and that is enough to give any memory false encouragement and suddenly they are all clamoring for my attention, each with the bland color of ill-timed events. Where to hide during the storm of recollections? To hide at all? I will try to hide.

Frank has dementia. A perpetual storm of bland memories behind his eyes, I presume. I am the only one who knows this around here. Too little discipline, I saw it would happen. For exercise I flex my versatility upon the present. I can still do that. I balloon the now into some sort of event and get to work on examining its details. Then—and I say this without strict presumption—the right memory emerges and I drop it into the center of now for a preliminary inspection.

Plop.

But by no means will I leap after it and risk ambush following the bout of fear that drove me to hide in the present in the first place. Instead, when I am happy with its color I abandon the now once again. Do you see my plan for progression? The built-in safeguards to floundering? How telling you about my plans is another safeguard? If only you knew how presumptuous, how cocky, these words make me seem to myself, and how easy it could be for me to be so, you would marvel at my self-deception, my immense effort to be something else.

But you see I do not want to be marvelous. Not any more. Just reliable. Reliable enough to be heard for the time it takes to lay out the correctly–colored facts for your judgment and, if there be any owed me, punishment. For what have I to fear now, here, at my age, after what has happened to me, a star so far from the eyes I imagine might recognize me, and besides whose light, by the time it is seen, by those who are strangers to me, will have gone out?

Only insanity, which I pick my way gingerly around each day.

Hunger makes good colorful sauce. I have seen Frank eat and then lounge listlessly on the rattan, slow as Loris, smugly certain death, when it comes, will arrive too late to cause him any distress. Another one for whom each day is a gift. I line up a battalion of objections but exercise none of them, unsure of whether, once going, I could spare him his life, deprive him of more gifts. I am glad of him, though, he is one of my aides against insanity. He is—I am sorry for more money talk—a benchmark. A low-water mark. If I were Frank I could not go on; so long as I know I am not Frank I find I can. Thank you Frank. Fuck you Frank. From Frank I draw inspiration.

Let me try this. The closest I can get, with this high stippled sky, metallic water, and the ring of steel against steel, is Cologne and the Rhine in late October, colder than you may think. *Viel arbeit* but *viele leute* as well, streaming in from the East, Frank-lazy and with special privileges not open to Eoin, who at this time needs a dentist, among other things. One week earlier, a replica sky has welcomed him into Zeebrugge, drunk from the chase across a choppy channel. Yes, we can leave the now, for now, and follow Eoin's trail to continental Europe, some, but not many, years after the meeting with Brophy and Devlin in wintry Leeds.

*   *   *

The officials search the Volkswagen that fresh morning and ask Eoin where he is from and where he is headed, and for what purpose. To dispute one, unavoidably leads to certain other, classifications one must ineluctably contend with, a wise man might tell you. Being born a human is one. Let us start there, for argument sake.

If you develop an inkling you are not a human, it is all very well to toy, but try to make the claim and you will quickly see how impossible it is to claim anything at all, above all that you are distinct from humanness. Being specifically a man or a woman is another you cannot expect to overcome though I will allow there is more room for topographical tampering. When you think of everything else, right down to your family, whose word you have to take for that fact, and you see how much is uncertain, it is hard to face a port official with relatively few years of life remaining with any degree of sincerity. He expects a simple lie.

Eoin finds something to say and, careful to keep to the right, drives inland.

Later that same day he arrives in Yypres and, after walking around for hours returns to his car just before dark and vomits, in a logical conclusion to the rising nausea and swelling stomach that has been confusing his thoughts since morning. It could have been the curled port sandwich or simply all the new ideas. It did not matter to him which, in the end, in the throes of it.

Spirits of dead soldiers, wise now, console him each time he stops his breathing, and has to cough up the last cupful of air to get it going again. All the while he can hear their low encouragement, feel them pat his back lightly. He must look something like a crow chick now, fallen from its nest, to the millions of eyes peering up from beneath the earth at him, bawling downwards to them, for some sort of comfort.

Nothing one can do sometimes to help oneself but wait. It is a time for falling back on something.

In the swirling delirium he eats the brown Flanders soil to nourish, he believes, his depleted body. It is hot with garlic, gorgeous; muddy like burdock, and gritty goes without saying, but no more than airborne sand in a beach sandwich, he finds. Or a dirty prawn. What stones he comes across are large and easy to avoid putting in his mouth. The grass haulms that he reefs up to reach the soil beneath have swellings at the root-tops that gleam at him through the dewy darkness. The tears he justifies by eating the torn roots. For even out of his usual mind he still hears his father's advice:

'Only kill what you can eat.'

'Yes, Da. I know.'

The masticated cud never stays down for long. An impasto of Belgian milk, mud and roots has to be repeatedly disgorged. But this does not interfere with the work. He goes on eating. There is plenty of milk—most of a gallon—though they think in terms of liters here in Belgium, he corrects himself quickly. The sooner he gets used to the differences the better, he thinks, then goes back to eating. Somewhere below the torn-off roots are wild potatoes, he is sure of it. Small, translucent pearls, sweet enough to eat raw and an instant cure for disorientation. He rips and digs, and what he rips and digs he eats with milk, and presently expunges, all in a steady flow of honest to goodness effort.

'Good boy. This is my boy, Eoin. Eoin this is my friend Mac. He is still a bit sleepy, Mac, he'll be alright in a second. Eoin, show Mac your muscles. Eoin, show Mac how you. . . how you. . . how you find potatoes in Yypres. Where? Now, you know well where they are! Don't have me to get up to you now. Stop messing around now, remember what I told you. Don't have me to repeat it, now. Now.'

'Yes, Da. I remember now. I remember.'

'Good boy.'

Bits of soil grit get compacted inside the cavity shaft running through the center of one molar until the knifing pain is too frightful and, though ashamed of quitting, he gives up biting to obey this new and sobering master of pain.

The following day Eoin sleeps in the car and begins to feel more at ease. The day after, he leaves Yypres, heading for Germany. He carries with him grains of soil, tucked inside his pulsating tooth. He thanks his lucky stars for that small mercy. He can worry about what to do next in smaller intervals. Each second is now roomier as the present slides more slowly by. So long as he has his tooth he feels sheltered from other troubles.

'Claire, Aaron . . .I don't know what to say. I made it across. It's grand and . . . well they all drive like lunatics. . . like you Claire. . .Ha ha! I know what. . .I know where you get it from now. They gave me a bit of hassle at the port over the lights. You never warned me! Anyway I told them I'd get yellow ones. See what happens here in Germany. Just crossed the border this morning, should be in Cologne tonight. I'll tell you all about it in the next. . . eh. . .dispatch? I found Yypres, it was like you said. I hope your great grandfather is looking over me know. It smelled like Ireland, you were right. It smelled like thyme, I swear. I know Aaron is laughing his head off. That's T-H-Y-M-E son. Fields of thyme. When I woke up the air was thick with the smell and the land looked like a gardener was gathering in armfuls of holy smoke laid down during the night to protect the dead from the living. The smoke had the smell of thyme. It was gone when the sun came up and I wanted to smell it again and walk through the smell so I stayed another day. But. . .then I headed off. We'll all go there together next time. I'm going to look for a dentist in Cologne. Maybe I can find something out at the employment office. I think I'll be at least one tooth lighter next time you see me. Have they tooth fairies here? Ha ha! I hope so. All I could think of was The Marathon Man when I heard the petrol station man talking. Everything in German sounds like a threat. Ha ha! I'm getting used to it though. I'll be at the hostel before it gets dark. I know everything will be alright. I have a good feeling but I miss you both and wish I could turn around and go back, even after all we talked about. After landing here, after seeing Yypres, things appear different. It's a big world! Bigger than you think! The last thing, I almost forgot. I saw a kid, a toddler, falling over yesterday on the gravel. It was a funny thing. You know how when kids fall they don't know if they are hurt enough to panic and cry until they look at an adult's face. They think that even the sensation of getting hurt is for somebody else to decide, or to give them permission; they are so dependent for everything. Well it occurred to me it's the same for some adults, soldiers for instance. They say you should never allow the wounded to see the horror on your face or else they will give up and lose the will to stay alive. Isn't it true we can put up with all sorts so long as we have nobody to tell us how badly off we are? We can tolerate any present pain, once our eyes are on something different, something that doesn't care about our pain. Because pity is terrifying when it is aimed toward you. It makes you give up and cry. Bang, bang, bang! Ha ha! Anyway the toddler didn't cry, but I expected it to, until I saw its mother's face myself. Lucky it didn't see mine I guess. Ha ha! Time to speaka di Deutch folks. Over and out. Your spy in Europe. Herr Owing.'

The stop button is wide as a piano key.

Up there, way up in the dusty sky, he can see where the American fire bombs came from that charred and gutted the city and left standing the big black cathedral, standing for war on a bulge of ground over the wide Rhine. It sends him a stark reminder that he is in a foreign country, and gives him an idea of what foreign might really mean: not yours, somebody else's. Twists of barbed spire reaching through the bed of new city concrete appear like delicate shoots, from the window of his hostel room. The breakfast token he holds in his hand is the first piece of currency given to him in Germany. *Frühstück* is printed on the rectangle of paper. An invitation to trust somebody to honor what he imagines is promised and yet still there is his end to keep up; he has to be there during the set time, be ready for a surprise system of obtaining food and, above all, be able to recognize the food the token entitles him to. That and the thought of going hungry, through an incapacity to connect this token with any secure image of a meal, yet unable to discard and forget it, puts him in a new state of blind anticipation.

Before, Eoin had the simple, arbitrary goal of reaching Cologne. Now here, the woollier business of living has begun to importune. Yet, he believes, with enough worry, that problem could be broken down into a series of lesser goals and tackled in a logical order according to the natural laws of human action under duress.

Soon after dusk it starts raining. A central heater whirrs and silent steam climbs the window and seems to conspire with the night. He wonders if he deserves to go to sleep early and resume responsibility tomorrow. He has walked enough today, he tells himself. The day is dead now, to profit at least; to sense. He gets into bed. He allows himself to go to sleep.

'*Mensch!*' A voice rings out between midnight and dawn. '*Mensch!*' A wolf barking back at the darkness, alone and speculative, a slowly revolving lighthouse beam. It does not wake him though he hears it clearly, just hurries his dreaming along through the gloom:

'*Where abouts?*' asks Eoin.

'*Oh,*' she says, opening not bloodshot but bleeding eyes, and with a shy expression on her old face that is an imitation of some odd child, '*everywhere.*'

Very slowly she barely presses her fingertips against several random points on her own body, through her clothes, as if to make sure. Each feather-light touch causes her to wilt a little more. The pain has worsened and spread, yet as it has done, her resistance to it, never declamatory anyway, fades more and more into fateful resignation. She will not go to the hospital nor see anybody except the boy. He has not the heart to ask her again if he should bring the doctor. He has not the heart to upset her tranquility with an outsider's words and the possibility of careless hope.

'I see you got a new washing machine at last,' he says then, for no special reason, while looking around, trying to remember the place and noting the changes since his last visit, 'you don't need to wash by hand anymore.'

'Ah sure, I have that years now. It's grand so it is,' she says, and then adds, 'You were right, Eoin, when you told me.'

He does not know what to say next. Hasn't he seen this washing machine before? Has it been so long? There are other things new to him as well but he does not mention them.

'I'll go and heat up some soup,' he says.

'Grand,' she says, and her eyes begin to close.

When he comes back from the kitchen the sitting room is empty and the hall door open. Outside in the small weedy garden sparrows are flitting around his mother. Her face is pointing toward the autumn evening sun that pours its fierce heat through a split in the charcoal rain-clouds. She is lying on her back and smiling a new smile.

'I'm grand,' she says, opening her eyes when he kneels beside her and says her name, and asks her another question because questions are easiest. 'I'm grand here.' Then she closes her eyes again. He does not try to move her.

He knows when she is gone by the sparrows.

He would have gone with her then, he feels, rather than this.

What causes him to wake up, as dawn is breaking, nobody will ever know. '*Mensch*!' has stopped. But before he understands his whereabouts—and it matters not that it is just a fraction of a second before—he recognizes the side of the world that has so far been faithful to him wherever he has awoken from the night. It has given him light every time he expected light. Now, swallowing the imperfect foreground of Cologne, dawn is cracking open, vaster than any before. Yes, he remembers, he is in Cologne, in Germany, in a hostel, in a room with a strange man. Details both clear and small. The bigger facts, like dawns, remain unperturbed. He can breathe easily. Dawns would survive, he believed, outlive all the minor details, and so would he.

The hump of a Leipziger's body, wrapped tightly in a thin white sheet, lies in the bottom bunk. It moos. Four sooty toes, and a hank of sandy hair at the opposite end, are all the visual evidence that a human can be recomposed from. All else, including the clothes pile and curled-toe ankle boots is circumstantial.

Two. At least they are not three. Imagining potential dialogues for later gives him the desired air of purpose for walking to breakfast. Through the watery wobble of a glass harmonica recording pairs of muscular morning eyes swim toward him as he approaches the reception desk. Down the end of a side corridor, a window appears, and through it brightness and thrashing trees disowning their sodden leaves as though to punish them for the miserable night that has passed. The leafy matter glides, helicopters down, and sinks onto the German *terrum* in waves of naïveté.

Each leaf only had to do it once. So had he. He only has to do this day once. Tomorrow, everything would be arranged differently, regardless of whether he spun, floated or dropped straight down to this day's end. He feels his soul pressing back, it is enough encouragement. *Weitargehen.*

The breakfast salami on his breath makes him feel cheap and worthless when his turn finally comes to enter the employment clerk's office, and among the grey-brown plastics of the *Arbeitsamt* she beckons to him like an orchid. A low-cut sleeveless sweater, tanned cleavage and red nails. Her bare, slender arms hung with bangles. A droplet of green crystal on a chain around her neck matches her eyes. Her straight hair is the weathered-blonde of sun-bleached wicker. Behind her pale lips, her teeth are as white as sea-shell. Only her nose seems at odds; it is large with a brief widening stamped on the bridge, from where it cuts down with a warrior's honesty. The nose and the rest are like blue and orange. Ahead of him is her image, surrounding it and flapping for attention, are countless others, wherever he shifts his eyes.

'Can you wax floors?' she says. Or so it seems to Eoin's ears at first.

'Can you speak English?' is his reply. She can and she is gracious and tells him which sites are hiring, explains the rigmarole of registering as a foreign resident, as a job seeker and, when the time comes, as a tax-paying worker. He did plan to stay longer than three months, did he not? For sure. He is wondering about: a) her height, and b) what she is wearing below the margin of the desk while all the while embarrassed because he has not much more to say to her in English than he had in German and because his breath is contending with her perfume and winning easily, befouling the citrusy office air with horrible efficiency. Honestly, only now does he think of Brophy and then he does not have to try hard to imagine evil most placid before incorruptible beauty.

Out from the tangle of hair on her head the memory of the mistress comes to bear against that of Brophy. Eoin's thoughts run from where the Frau lives, how and with whom, to what she is wondering about him in turn based on his appearance.

How much of his curiosity is reciprocated? His thoughts run right up to the hard contours of who she really is, to what extent she is naturally shaped to them, or can bend; no ultimate distinction there, no distinction ever probably. It is probably my error to suggest a distinction might exist. A falsehood. Be aware, my love, but not afraid, of my errors. I confess again to fallibility with urgency. It is the property of the air we cannot live without to dry out our paint while we are still working it; a constant battle with available time for a satisfactory result. We rip into it while the going is good, errors and all, just because. Because the errors are tiny. And anyway, they point us in the direction of perfection as all good fools do. Come with me now to meet some good fools, symbols of universal error, in Africa before today's paint dries up. For the love of fools come with me! There is still time before the workday ends and the cheers of liberation run toward the ever-waiting sea.

Come! Before my paint dries up.

SEVENTEEN

Jap was the name the commander in Africa went by. He was not Dutch, or Afrikaner. Nobody said Yaap, not even the Dutch or Afrikaners. What everyone said sounded more or less like Jyap, except a Corsican who said Shapuh with a blubber-lipped pout as though—Jap would say in his flat tone—offering to suck his cock. Ha ha! Napoleon himself laughed the loudest. If you want to know what I thought at last, I thought he was Irish. But without a face I had to go by his arms and hands. As for his behavior, Jap had evolved. . .well, we shall see. His voice, a surgical intervention, only confused matters. The only time his teeth, barely harmed by the chemical, were covered was when, with obvious discomfort, he pulled on a cigarette. The fibrotic rim of his mouth cavity made a poor substitute for lips. A leak of fresh air contaminated each lungful of smoke. No wonder he hated Napoleon with his succulent lips.

Hail the size of golf balls was hammering down on the corrugated iron sheltering us all when Jap shot Napoleon after what appeared to be a characteristically rapid decision. The first thing he took from the body was Napoleon's rabbit's foot. He put it in his own pocket. Up there, in upland Africa, he must have felt like *El Sordo*, the hum of approaching bombers inside his head inexorable. He was not going to make his last stand on an empty stomach. We had eaten as much meat as we could from the last skittish cow while it remained alive. Then we gorged in the race against the rot that took a matter of hours.

But now, hungry again, that seemed like long ago.

'He's as hairy as a gorilla, what's the difference?' This from Jap to rouse the men from their silent, unpredictable thoughts. If we survived, I knew at that instant, how we remembered Napoleon would affect how we all remembered Africa and her contents, and vice-versa, including Jap. A fluid memory of the whole to pour over, to ponder with intelligence and time, and maybe settle, or bring to stagnation at least, once and for all, and privately.

To fuck! The fake gorilla eye could never be settled. Not without the power to understand the freak of nature capable of conceiving and executing such an idea and, outside of that, the source of inspiration and the circumstances permitting it. My way, the inch-by-inch approach to getting things understood, is an evolutionary leap from such paths to conception. I think about the man who had placed the prosthetic eye in the first gorilla we shot. I somehow imagine it was a man, but it really does not matter who it was because I also think he is dead now. It helps me to elevate my image of him, however short of his true stature that comes (I will use any device to get closer the mark). In the end that man surely died of originality. An adventitious offshoot overwhelmed by his ability to be overwhelmed by the aimlessness of all others' actions. Before each breach of his own inactivity, the horror of repetition poised above his prone neck like an axe, impatient to drop.

No, I cannot understand him yet, and Africa flows on in my memory. As a result, dead Napoleon gets remembered afresh, as distinct from Jap's dead gorilla. As Eoin does.

*   *   *

Vile hands (What? Can I not say what I need to say, at my age? Of course I do not know why, not yet. Do you believe you will know at your end? Know more is all I can promise about mine. Knowing is in the lap of the gods.) and ultimatums, I find, go han… go together. Perhaps there is some genetic linkage. 'Live or die.' 'You decide.' 'It's up to you.' You know the tough-speaker's words, and you know his hands: priceless porcelain. The creamy curves of mock-innocence, always smaller than you expected, shy of moving or touching anything but each other. Clammy from hanging too closely. The fingers are amphibian. They will flex independently under water, only rest and occasionally flicker their tips in air.

My is not here today. I miss her. We are full of the food she left for us. Frank ate it like a dog. Too much, no self-control. Pandan cake after pandan cake. It is the first day without her. It has been terrible so far. My knee is killing me. It misses My too.

There are other care staff here but to tell the truth, I have paid no attention to them until today. They are no more than strangers to me. They could be as good as My, but I dread to have to take that chance. My is more than enough. But now she is not here I begin to notice different things, notice the same things differently. Some things, I believe, have the potential to be loved, eventually. But there are others, it seems, that can only ever be despised. Frank's hands for instance, his vile hands. Today I notice how his fingers appear to huddle ethnocentrically. Before picking something up they brush suspiciously, in a bunch, against it first.

'I'm going to a disco, Papa.'

I wish she had not mentioned where she was going. Disco is a word I taught her. I would not have believed the trouble it is causing me now. Draining equatorial water over again. Does the world, spinning on its axis, still have discos? Do sweet, loving girls still find happiness in discos, despite everything else that goes on? Do I hope so? I am afraid to ask but since I have to I have to be a Belgian port official about it, given the time remaining, and all that must be done if I am ever to be augured again. I will not be augured is something I cannot say today. What did I tell you before? I will not be augured? Yes, I was speaking about the immediate future; the projected duration of a mood, you understand, a spell of time. But I did not know you back then as well as I do now. All I said about loving you was put on, more of a lure than a lie because I knew I would love you in time. And I was right! I do! Can you not feel it sloshing off the page? Back then I did not bother to tell you my complete hopes for the future. You had not earned the privilege. But you needed to know how inflexible I could be. That is important. But you know the inflexible ones, let me tell you they are not always inflexible. Rubber sheets at times. Some of those times they are open to any offer of kindness, of respect. But you know, yes, you know. You know what I mean. You know me now, do you not? I do not have to treat you like a child, do I, explaining everything? For who knows better about how to give kindness and respect than one like me, one who never takes it for granted, measures every grain like a miser.

My will come back, and then, though I have not exactly stopped loving her, I will love her again. Love her afresh. Anything can happen, you know. Though it is madness to expect something to reassemble to its prior shape, once disassembled. I am not saying it is impossible. Just do not expect it. I am not mad. Not like the dozing glutton with vile hands beside me on the rattan. My is gone now and that is the plain truth. Her return is a supposition. It is a possibility that if you wish, you can render, however unmeritoriously, into future fact. But there are no such things as future facts, past and present only. Present only if you want the purest truth, the first press. My truth, that is. Around it a coronal haze that is pretty in paintings, certain stories, useful for dreaming.

If you dream.

I might have gone to the disco with her if I had not been thinking of you, my love, to keep an eye on her. What would they have made of me there I wonder? There would surely have been some local amputees.

How would they dance? I would not try to dance, of course, just lean against the counter sipping reeking spirits like a younger me, and keeping an eye out, also like a younger me. Like a proprietor.

Below my waist would be in shadow, I would make sure of it. A thread of fairy lights gilding the bar top and dance floor would be all there is to reveal my face to them. Electricity is not squandered in this country. No complaints from me. Perhaps nobody would notice me. I am sure now she would have liked me to go with her, though I never realized it when she was telling me. I do not know where it is exactly. She told me but I was dazed from what I had just heard. All I can recall is that it is somewhere along the road to Sihanoukville. The first bus back is at ten a.m. Why did she tell me that and not say she would be on it? I was waiting to hear where she would be sleeping but nothing. I was on the verge of asking. And her child, what about him? 'He is being looked after.' She told me that for some reason. Maybe she thought it was enough to quash my concern. I am a good actor when I want to be. I can spot good acting too. To pause or to continue tears at my nerves. If I stop…no it is not going to be another stop. Not now. I have stopped stopping. What is the value of a pause? A lazy aphid? Less than a mad woman's shite? No, I will continue, eschew the pause, abandon My to the disco, and hide from you the outer region of today's coronal haze, my dear.

EIGHTEEN

During the night coils of desultory light from the waning moon touch, and reveal, glinting tangents upon the water. The wet lapping of tame sea-tongues underwhelms my impatience for urgent change. But it seems tonight the sea shall do as it pleases. It will not be augured, at least not by me. I must empathize. Perhaps it is fulfilling Frank's or the will of some other who is unknown to me. Yet maybe it is mine after all. I could be kidding myself, working up this so-called impatience as a distraction, hoping it will infect something or somebody else, give me a distraught companion to love, to pity. Yes, maybe I am as calm as this endless tremulous dance floor, with its sparse boated fairy lights calling for me—the bravest of the brave—to step out and inspire the timider to follow, only for me to despise them for allowing me be their leader. Leave my wisdom behind to despise them, rather, for by then I will be forever dancing in a split moment of pure distraction and no longer caring.

Why should I care about Eoin, or any of the rest of them? They have done me no good. Pulling myself back each day to these memories is a stupid compulsion. An augured fool, no matter what I tell you otherwise. Can I not stop and stay stopped? No more stop, unstop; unstop, stop? Augur myself once and for all? Can I not cut the sound, the light, the smell, and the touch? I wonder which goes first, which is last to go? I imagine it is touch, the light last. There is always light, even in sleep. Smell and sound can scrap for second. Imbeciles. But where is the anger to self-augur in this way? Who will inspire me here with enough anger, enough revulsion? Inspire *me*! I am *not* Frank!

*   *   *

Eoin, the poor little bastard, feels fortunate to have met Frau Graber on his first proper day in Cologne. It appears to bode well for his future. An optimist, he decides to place that short interview at the *Arbeitsamt* as the launch pad for his new life. From now on, he has merely to build upon, or maintain the momentum she has imparted to him: a beautiful, opulent, healthful model for his Germany life.

Alcohol had begun to excite his mind with possibilities long before he left Ireland for Manchester, and he is well aware of its potential. Alcohol alone might be enough, he had sometimes felt, when he was in a reducing mood. *Reductio ad absurdum.* Then poof! sometime later absurdity overcame him. But just before then, the simplicity of a one at its peak of oneness; during that instant before the idea fractures, before one must start all over again from scratch, scavenging, preferring *hue* to *color* and such rubbish until one's confidence is strong enough not to care again, even *to not care*, not caring about defunct grammar rules either, sacredly permitting all errors if they really are errors at all, for who knows what they will be later, or what else will have become defunct when, on the final day, the ultimate day when tomorrow is the only certain error, all acts are lined up and the classification of the whole is made, in a hurry, the remaining seconds too precious, laughably precious, to waste. When what matters 'at the end of the day' is, finally, truly known.

The alcohol fumes that fill the hostel room when Eoin returns worn out again, this time from searching for but not finding Frau Graber's dentist, are not guilty of abruptly upsetting, with unpleasant thoughts, the digestion of his late lunch taken in the park with the pigeons. Rather, it is the white envelope lying on the fold of his sleeping bag, licked-stuck, that triggers the pang.

When the police, the army, the enemy (name your own organized opponents, I have no intention of splitting hairs with you) loose canisters of gas that twizzle and hiss out poison, you know something new has started. A new phase has been announced, prettily enough withal. A mere moment after seeing the letter, 'Al-lo-o' comes the voice from below with parabolic intonation, unmistakably mocking, even without the after-titter. The Leipziger has a full head now and a face, configured by the same chance that extends, unabashedly, to what might loosely be termed his entire life. In preference to despairing, he is a man who instead celebrates his impotence before chance's might each new day with a drink.

This day has been comfortingly ordinary so far for the German, each passed hour a lightening of the morning's brutal burden. Just before midnight, stripped down to a mere spirit, he will levitate and, from a height see, clearest, manifold essences, and laugh. Then after cries of '*Mensch!*' periodically issued through the night, he will fall asleep sometime before dawn.

At the moment he is shelling peanuts on a yellow thumbnail. Escaping flakes sprinkle on to his body, naked but for the bed sheet I have already mentioned. The head dips under the upper bunk frame, birdlike, to better peer from its roost. Meanwhile, in yellow ink, Eoin very slowly and silently reads: *Call home* — possess — *urgently* — possess yourself — *you have gone far enough* — possess your own self and your world – *we must have you back* – possess your own self and your own world — *all will be forgiven* — possess your forgiveness — *do not make us have to change your mind* — possess your own forgiveness —...

...— be your own man.

The German either expects to be ignored, and so holds his peace for a few more nutshelling moments or, as he is well over halfway to the spiritual crack-out, is growing prudent lest his levitation be endangered by a wayward word or act.

The extent of Eoin's indifference to him, however, were he to fully grasp it, would surprise him. The German, no doubt aware of his own conquered fear and the charisma this lends him, assumes it is put on. He is unable to fathom that he is merely part of the warm palpitating sound that seems to exist, out of spite, almost everywhere Eoin finds people. The German is not odd, to Eoin, but common. A label we all feel entitled to refuse.

'*Kein arbeit heute*?' again the exaggerated looping, the mockery.

'Orientation,' from Eoin, 'post-Nazi orientation. Work tomorrow maybe.'

'*Englisch*?'

Eoin is reading the letter again, gleaning clues, constructing scenarios like wildfire. E.T. call home. Cretins. He looks away from the note and bends down. He looks intently at the German's face to see if there is even the faintest resemblance to somebody, even some*thing*, he has known. The abrupt attention flatters, and then begins to unsettle the other. Who knows what or why Eoin seeks something there but he finds nothing special, a bushman perhaps, a gorilla with two natural eyes, a fragment of the noisome whole without special distinction.

It might have stirred his respect, that appraisal, had the German presumed it correctly. Maybe even love. But the first hurdle, pretension, is a stubborn cunt. When she flashes her grin, and stands in one's path with a single raised eyebrow, hands to hips, all presumption is barred. One demands raw data, at all costs, to clear a path. The wordless look leaves the German dissatisfied. He expires protractedly and loudly, then slurps *Kölsch* from his can. He farts too, I believe. He is just raising the belch, working out his plan, when, on the climb to his bunk, Eoin crushes his shelling hand against his bedframe with the chunky sole of a workboot, hardly sensing the vile gristle.

'*Mensch*!'

All the lovely ladies smile at once and the world is at ease again. Dreamtime for Eoin. His crack-out.

*   *   *

One wish (wishing time first). Of all the things one would change, which one first? Tongue-tied.

Eoin would have untied his tongue, and told the mistress the details about his father's visit, what he had said about her, what he had implied, the news he had brought with him, his advice, the failed attempted beating that became a taunt to be beaten, then the abrupt switch to conciliation when his father heard the mistress's car pull up outside.

But before that he would have told her about the old struggles; what he knew she wanted to hear. She had called the police anyway. Keeping quiet had not prevented that.

He was fourteen, his father reminded him, he could do as he pleased. He was a man, finally. The mistress had an expectation of Eoin, but until his father showed up, brazenly, at her house that day while she was out, neither Eoin nor she had confronted it with a word. A psychologist might choose a different term, but loyalty was expected. To her over his father.

Eoin's father, like all fathers, was owed it.

He timed the visit nicely, making the journey by bus and then, just after the last rain shower, travelling on foot the remainder of the way, managing not to get wet. His footsteps rang clear, delighting and exciting the birds that were all achirp in the day's final, freed rays of daylight. Those sounds seemed to be in harmony with a decent if overly bouncy and heavy left-handed nocturne that carried through the window of the house and floated out on to the street outside.

A mucous of algae clung to the roots of isoponic plants in glass globes strung with wire from the porch ceiling. Only the idea would have held any interest for Eoin's father. He had managed to pull himself together, as he always could in public, even when the worst had occurred. In private, control was impossible for even the smallest problems.

Wood smell. The fragrance of that wooden piano, inside, beneath the lid, bathing the hammers and wires, and wafting off the polished rosewood exterior. The extravagant detail. The smell of rot-resistant beauty. And all that even before the sound of the notes. The miracle of transportation from his trapped mind had Eoin typically mesmerized at the moment his almost forgotten father pressed a trigger finger against the bell button. Eoin stopped playing to answer the door.

They were saying goodbye on the porch under the plants when the mistress had removed the last of the shopping bags from the car and pushed the boot-door shut with an elbow. She started the instant the man's eyes met hers. His reaction to her shouting—if it could be called a reaction—was to invent words that seemed to be for Eoin but were in fact meant for the mistress.

'I have to go now, son. Remember what I told you. Remember now!' He raised his voice and wagged a finger with the final words. A red rag. She even stomped a foot. She could have killed him, that worthless man. But restraint prevailed. She could not become him and, by that peculiar and catastrophic process, he her.

Instead of killing him, instead of talking about him, she first took a bath and thought about him. There were three of them in it and she too must have known by now how that was a bad number. Of course he knew where Eoin was living, his type knew where everyone lived.

But she did not know where he lived, and with what tenderness the alleged death of Eoin's mother hours earlier, during the thunder and showers, had been described:

'Yes, son, she came back to me, so she did. It was soon after you left me, thank God. But she was not well, do you see? I had to look after her. She improved a little, but she was never really well again after you left her. She used to ask about you. I even fibbed to her and told her I'd been to see you, and that you were grand. She couldn't understand you'd been taken into another home and that meant we weren't allowed to visit. She said that one of us visiting you was enough, and that she preferred it be me. I was afraid to upset your new life, so I didn't come to you, and I made up news for her. But the two of us, we missed you son. We would have loved to have you back with us, in our little auld home; it's nothing compared with this pace, no fancy piano, but it's your home. *Your home.* And always will be.'

Just before he took a swipe at Eoin he had added: 'we might have gone to Rush together again.'

Eoin was not silent the whole time. But when he began to speak it lacked something, impact or weight, and always brought about the same reply: 'Yes, yes I know,' his father would say. 'Yes son. Yes, I know.'

Smothering.

Until it silenced him up and his father managed to take offence.

Later, the mistress was not able to recognize the loyalty Eoin had paid to her, the disloyalty to his father, that lay in not accompanying him *home* to see his mother's putative corpse; his loyalty to the mistress had manifested as a skepticism, and somehow survived among the debris of his trampled feelings. Had his father told him his mother was still alive, though, it would have been different. But what the mistress fixated on was his galling silence, a treacherous silence for her. She had to break it down, or accept that seven years of care had been in vain. That was the ultimatum she set for herself.

The other things his father talked about before attacking Eoin were coming of age, and about work and the road to self-reliance, and a little about women and their wants, then about the mistress in particular. A higgledy-piggledy homily unlike anything he had heard in seven years. 'Life is closing in,' he said, 'your plane is just lifting off. Mine has landed. Your mother's has docked in the terminal.' He used a train metaphor too: life was racing past, to be grabbed and carriages bitten off. As he grabbed and took a broken-toothed bite from a passing train he seemed to get carried away. He shut his eyes and then stumbled across the mallard-green living-room carpet. His eyes were slow to re-open and then his face had a strange expression. He seemed to have forgotten what he was saying, and who Eoin was.

That is when Eoin realized he had been drinking, and that somehow he had managed to seem sober up to that point. When Eoin steadied him, it served to remind the man of the hurt this boy had caused him, and his ring connected with one of Eoin's canine teeth, loosening it.

In contrast to himself, the mistress smelt him the instant she entered the house, Eoin knew, before she saw the broken items on the floor. She said nothing about them, and so there was nothing he could do about that but feel shame for what another one of his family had brought upon her.

'He's gone now. Don't worry,' was all she said, and put her arms around him, 'I'll make sure he never comes back.'

She was confused in her thinking though. She seemed to see Eoin's father's visit as an irregular incident, perhaps like any other average adult might have seen it. It is possibly how you see it, too. One of life's rogue happenings that, like a hail shower, or a pipe-bomb, are spurious, out of the ordinary, and can be disregarded as not being a regular concern. If struck without being killed, one managed to get over it somehow, believe that one would not be struck again, resume normal life.

It was initially inconceivable to the mistress that Eoin's father's visit had, in fact, closed the loop on another spurious incident. The incident of living with the mistress that had lasted for seven years.

NINETEEN

Brown creekwater drew semi-tame deer to the grounds of a sprawling Colorado house. The owner of the estate, a Mexican chemist and ex-volunteer fireman called Gomez, sent me to Africa. His money sent me, to be more precise. It was not right what was going on there, to his way of thinking, he told me.

'Fuck Mexico! I shit in her mother's milk.' He was a born dreamer. He would not lift a finger for Mexico, out of revenge. But Africa broke his heart, he said, and he could not explain, did not care that he could not explain, why. The mere word was enough to start him off.

He was putting another band together to try again and he wanted me in it. There were to be no Americans, North or South. He hated the Americans.

'There are lazy. Every single motherfucker,' he said, brandishing a hickory stick at a dozing buck in our path. It made a scene then cleared off and Gomez laughed and swore after it, lovingly, like it was his son.

'What comes first, the urge to e-shit or the idea?' he said as we walked.

'I...'

'Don't think about it, just give me your answer. Which comes first?'

'They come at the same time.'

'The urge to e-shit,' said Gomez without seeming to be too disappointed with my response. He ruminated awhile, carefully beating a dense spreading weed out of the hoof-marked lawn with the end of his stick. 'But they can seem to happen at the same time,' he conceded to me at last.

We talked freely in the warm April rays, cut through thinly by irregular icy gusts from the Rockies. I remember it was April because he said no more snow this year, and there was an old pile turned brown, melting on the shaded creek-bank. When Gomez said something, the sounds and movements from the world around him, even the spiraling of eagles high in the sky, returned strenuous affirmation. The span of perceivable world around his house was at intense, secure, peace under his aegis, and compared with his account of his past, so was he.

'You only have one chance to do a thing,' he repeatedly said to me, with the pointedness of a father. 'You must act with a full heart, think later when you are useless for anything else. Then you will have something worthwhile to think about.'

We took the roasted venison outside with plenty of salt for seasoning, and Mountain Dew, as his sons came and went from the table, interrupting our talk with impunity. It made no difference to me, they were his responsibility I remember thinking at the time, but if I were their father things would be different.

'They are not mine,' he said eventually, he must have sensed something from my attitude. '*De otro cabron*.'

He said he often talked to himself these days. The shame of it he revealed to me as well, perhaps unintentionally. There was nobody left to listen to that type of talk, he said. I imagined the type of talk he meant, not having a natural son and so on. But I was wrong. He had sons. He told me the next time we met, days before flying out. Natural ones. The exact head count as his adopted ones. In Mexico. Somewhere in Mexico. He had not been satisfied with them, back then. That too shamed him to admit. But he could not turn back the clock, go back. Time past was time set like concrete; you had to work with the fresh stuff, and work fast, he said by way of advice to me.

I loved the man.

*   *   *

I hate this place. Sometimes it feels like the best place I have ever been.

My back has long since furled like a winter leaf from a sawtooth oak, unable to fall. I remember the look in My's eyes now, on the day she left, like the look on the day I arrived here. Kind, yes, I suppose you would say kind, but with a coolness to it. How much I had put into winning her over. What a fool I had been. Each memory of her ridicules me. What did she really make of me? What did she tell her friends? I can see clearer now. The clarity is horrible. I had been too painstaking in the telling of my story.

'You have to write a story about you, and about Eoin,' she had said to me. Over again, I brushed her off. Who would read it? Who would be tricked to care?

I had loved her principled reaction.

'You must write the story. It is your duty.'

'To whom?'

'To you.'

And she had convinced me. She, a peasant girl unable to read, had convinced me that I would feel more a part of this world of people if I wrote the story. The possibilities. Yes, I ran away with myself into a realm of optimism, waged war on my health to revive it and I almost died of the fever, on top of everything else. But I did not die. And chance gave me sight of the treetops, and as I began to write my pages, and talk about them to My, I believed something was improving. I began to follow her gaze everywhere, and when time ripened enough I tottered a few steps from my bed to her lap. I even congratulated myself for doing so. When I think of it now! I am too ashamed to think of it. Breathing shames me so I try not to, and just listen to the heart inside that has been pumping away thoughtlessly all along.

'Look at the bastard I'm stuck with!' I know its new thinking. To move now, to move this ink around in time, it is the same as breathing. But I am not ready to make a scene. I want to plan my cessation, leave with an explored conscience, not as a confused fool beyond punishment.

Periodically I feel my body thicken, bracing itself for the approaching pain that it must endure all over again when a wrong path is diagnosed, and a new one for the future—yet another future—must be selected from the same list. It is a constant feeling now. How many have I selected and still must continue to pretend there is anything good remaining? How can I continue to follow the old system of choosing, over and over again?

I may yet love another here, in this place. In a few sentences, if I continue, I may change may to will. I will change may to will. I will love another here before I cease. But that is only a promise. The truth is that I may or I may not. It depends on so many factors, which in turn depend on who or what is love worthy. But closer to certainty, I am almost sure, is that if I am to live I must find something new to love. There it is laid bare, a twirl of my current predicament, a glimpse of the work that lies ahead. Another *before,* which mastery will one day convert to an *after,* then to repeat more masteries if I have not discovered a way out of the system by that time. What grounds do I have for supposing I may find a way out? None. But try getting that across to me! I prepare for a reluctant act instead. My love has to be consummated with an act. If only there were another way. 'Keep thinking while you write,' I tell myself. What will that act you dread be? What are the possibilities? Suddenly too many to think of, an endless list, and all of them I am poorly equipped to perform, so I had better prepare to make the effort flawless, make it thoroughly exhausting. Few can love a useless prick, none one who cannot be bothered to become exhausted by effort once something is underway. It will all come down to the bother. In preparation I must get ready to be greatly bothered with enthusiasm for the next love–capturing act I perform. Or turn traitor and join the ranks of my despisers and torture my heart with shallower and shallower breaths, threaten to blame it if it stops, for giving up on me. Those are just some of the options.

But can it not all be tied up somehow? The latest and final mastery, can it not be a tying up of all the ones that went before? Can I not love that alone, the tying up of all the rest? The tying up of me? Be frantically bothered by that one act, brushing aside the peripheral, the extraneous? None of this has anything to do with my love for you, by the way. That is a special love, precious and pure. It can never be broken. Remember that. Remember.

Not impure like my love for Gomez.

TWENTY

A day is beautiful when it subverts expectations. Or when you are able to forget that you are caught up in the endless guile of driving people back or coaxing them closer, so as to permit your passage around their obstructive lives. Jellyfish, sensitive as eyes, drift quietly in to shore some days. Compact and frictionless buttons, they become stranded and settle on the tidal belt. Nothing chews them on land, not even the black Alsatian, though I imagine it must be otherwise at sea where appetites are more subtly tuned.

At night the beached jellyfish reflect the light of the moon, as the moon shines from the sun that has become yesterday or will be tomorrow, diminuendo down to my own eyes. If I see that sun again, my negotiation of another full day will begin. Not until then will I rifle my memory for what I can use to bring about some deal.

You should see me when I imagine a clear scene of joy. I mean picture it in all its living dimensions at this very moment as if occurring in the next room or behind the stand of trees, perhaps in the new building that is going up. I can bring about a deal in minutes, even seconds! Then I rush off to that scene, rapt. I save hours on those days. Whole hours that, I hope, in the future I can put to some, different, use I have not yet thought of.

But, like everything else, days vary according to expectations—yours and others. And according to the future, according to what you have no grounds for presuming because it is not for you. *Not yours.* I must make you understand that. But you see the problem with all of this? A thing has to be now, or ago, to be; plans are permissible but the same plan must not be brought up twice. Later, if all conditions are met I may tell the rest of what I remember from Africa. Surely that would be a marriage for life. But we would have to be much surer of our mutual love before that.

*   *   *

At the very end of a deep inhalation, at the motionless moment before the air passes out again, Eoin catches a scent of gas. For reasons unknown to him, it is a smell he associates with Devlin. It now represents the slightly noxious emission from that fibrillating body. The other thing he discovers besides the note and the gaseous spoor, wrapped in a cloth and coated in a thin film of oil, is a well-maintained Browning that, for an instant and despite himself, he admires. A full magazine judging from its weight. He does not need to check. He puts it back inside the sleeping bag and gets in alongside it, then off to sleep with him.

When he awakens it is dark outside, late evening. There may well be people who, by their very nature, feel safe and protected by the cloak of nightfall. Or there may be only occasions when they feel so. Somebody may research the subject one day. Yet how private the night! How respectful of privacy! How confidential!

Immediately upon waking Eoin hears a rustle and, remembering the pistol, thinks about shooting the Leipziger through *Das Bild* that would be shielding his torso. But it is simply one of those passing thoughts to keep the conscience on its guard. Where would one be without them? Another thought is just to point the gun at him to see his reaction. He climbs down from his bunk.

Browning pistols are quite big and, with a full magazine, heavy. Eoin holsters it the best he can inside his jacket, not caring whether the German lowers his newspaper and sees him working out the best arrangement for carrying it. Finally he settles for butt-first, with the barrel aiming upwards at an angle across his heart though it might make for a slow retrieval.

Ha ha! He has to laugh then at the obviousness of the current solution to his tangle of actions and thoughts. Everything has fallen into place for him again, even in Cologne. Nothing can trouble him now except an interruption of kindness from the Germans. A foreign element. He has fallen on his feet.

How should he take his leave of the Leipziger? Perhaps bracing him with one hand behind the neck and tapping the muzzle gently against his temple, politely reissuing words already familiar to both of them for greatest intimacy: '*Kein arbeit heute*?' Then kissing him?

'No.' His mind speaks up again, after some consideration. When his gear is all packed up Eoin leaves the room and the hostel without goodbyes to anybody. He takes tomorrow's *frühstück* token with him. Nobody knows his plan, not even he. Finding nothing attached to the underside of the car, he rolls off slowly in search of a route southwards. He experiences an ecstasy of awareness.

An idea forming in his mind runs something like this: somewhere to the South I will escape my mistake. If not I will be fascinated to learn the extent of its reach.

Each mile pleases his heart like an honest Mark earned. He takes none for granted. At a *Raststätte* south of Wiesbaden in the early morning Eoin speaks into the tape recorder.

'...I walked across Dublin that night. I've never told you this before. I probably couldn't have walked that far during the day—you know how easy it is to walk a long way during the night, when you can't see too far ahead or around you, and you're feeling a bit nervous. I passed house after house where I imagined families were sleeping peacefully. As it was getting bright a smell of mushrooms drifted over a high wall and when it hit me that mushroom air also had a chill. I realized I was walking beside the Phoenix Park. I could see above the wall a line of treetops against the sky. When I thought about them later I found out they were chestnut trees. I came to a little revolving gate in the wall with grey peeling paint and I went in. I'd never been inside the Phoenix Park before. I remember it struck me as odd, very strange, that people had decided to keep a piece of land in the city where the rules—the park rules—were not the same as everywhere else. Not even the same as on land that looks similar in the country. Just like that they had decided. The zoo is in there, you know. It's where Aaron's parents live. He'll tell you all about it, Claire. Ha ha! I decided to walk all over the park, if necessary, until I found the zoo and then. . .well I wasn't really sure what I was going to do. Anyway I found it fairly quickly on account, first of all, of what I thought was a trumpeting elephant, and when I got closer to that sound I saw a signpost that said: Zoological Gardens. The road I was on, inside the park, was in rough condition and it turned out of sight, up ahead, toward the zoo. On either side of the road the old chestnut trees had rucked up the path and, beyond the trees, catching the early sun, a million dewdrops were spread over the grass that stood still and seemed to have sprouted overnight. I looked again at the sign that said Zoological Gardens in black ornamental lettering on a white background wet with dew that would have been glossy even if it was dry, and I thought: somebody has put that sign there to guide people to the zoo, and it will remain there until somebody takes it down—a different person. As I thought about the sign and its interference with my plans for finding the zoo on my own, I heard another call. I took it, from the timing of the sound, and the loudness, very personally—as something aimed at me. It came from a cock pheasant. It batted its wings as if it was too fat to fly anymore, using furious energy. It reached its body as tall as it could go without lifting its feet off the ground. Then it strutted out into a sort of glade of shorter grass that a shaft of sunlight missed by a few inches. I knew how much because of where it caught the pheasant's feathers, and set the colors alight like copper and green washing up liquid. Then the hens appeared, darting about him in the low shade, and I stood still for a long time that morning watching those pheasants in the phoenix park that nobody else could see. As I watched them I kept looking around for people. But there were only odd cars passing through the main avenue of the park that I could hear but wasn't able to see. I was hoping to see somebody. I was hoping that somebody would walk up to me, any other person, even the people who wanted me dead. It's a similar morning now. I can see flat fields covered in water for miles behind the petrol station. I'm moving to Berlin, they won't find me there. I'll stay at a backpackers hostel to start with. *Ich bin ein Berliner.*'

Eoin stops the machine and puts the tape in an envelope and drops it in what he thinks is a mailbox. He then continues toward the equator.

TWENTY ONE

Something I had planned to read aloud to My when I got to know her better.

My father's people were hunters from the North. For years I knew nothing about them. During the hunting season they camped, like Red Indians, on the floors of great glacial valleys that lay in shadow beneath bright mountaintops until mid morning. Before dawn the river's music awakened them. The children cried from the cold or hunger and the mothers were at their busiest; faith in their heritage was their source of vitality. They had borne or would bear children and those children's years were an extension of their lives: one endlessly growing and unbroken life. Each child's cry was a reminder to them.

The men walked several miles of riverbank in the breaking light to reconnoiter the coming day's weather and to absorb the morning magic of the unbound part of their lives. They ate breakfast when they returned and the women had settled the children and built the fires up. The water running freely past was a constant meditation on their thriving. The fatty beaver's tail, smoked, and potato stew seasoned with thyme and salt cooked quickly. Unlike in the evenings, they drank the river water cold in the mornings, drawing from it its icy energy. The younger children drank sour sheep's milk carried in bladders whose smell was to forever remind them of where they came from.

As the day whirled slowly open the men left the camp and walked up-river, yet further away from the distant Fjord that they had migrated from to hunt, to higher broken ground where animals could hide. Through pine stands they climbed twisting and ancient paths without maps. Silently, they separated into hunting pairs. They hunted all day, the last pair returning when the day stood on its head and the tree-less peaks were glowing, yellow through violet, from the western sun, and the valley had fallen again into shadow, burdened with game. Before eating the men cooled their snow-burnt faces in the river, pressing the palms of their hands into the golden sand it ran over, lifting a handful and scratching their skin with it for coarse relief. The woodsmoke and aroma from the evening's food would pool and waft with mounting intensity to their hunger senses.

During the day, while they men were away, the women cured the meat and scraped the hides in the dry valley air.

The men and women were siblings or cousins. As for the children at the hunting grounds, each knew a mother or a father or both. But their grandparents had each died, before being captured in their first grandchild's memory, on the fifth day after the birth. Only the childless could control their own fate and, to a lesser degree, the fate of their parents. Women who did not reproduce by their twenty-fifth year, and men by their thirtieth, were thereafter forbidden from doing so, and fated to be childless. The lives of the childless were tolerated but considered not worth living in the eyes of the fecund: they were held in contempt, as cowards and thieves are in all brave societies, and those individuals had to find their own, private, value in living. They were, however, free to die naturally.

It had to be either a natural life or a natural death.

The childless remained at home at the Fjord to tend the livestock during the hunting season.

Over dinner the men told of their day's hunt. They compared information on the movements of their quarry across the hunting grounds, debated its meaning for the future. For entertainment they were particularly interested in mishaps. For that they had to rely on a single account coming from the witness of the pair. It was correctly assumed that a tempered account was given, from which the rest of the men would construct a more likely scenario. Everyone enjoyed the tremendous mock-humiliation, laughter and ridicule that was staged over dinner. It excited the children very much. The women enjoyed the entertainment too but they were usually tired by this time and quiet, checking on the youngest children between serving their men.

When the food was eaten up they smoked an analgesic herb that abruptly switched their mood to communal melancholy. Only the men and the women smoked, that is to say the matched men and women who had produced children already. Under the influence of the drug, with the unintoxicated gathered around them, they would speak about their own parents, the dead grandparents of their sons and daughters. They spoke of them not as parents but as grandparents, though the office had lasted only five days. It was as if those five days were the most important, more valued than all the previous years they, or anyone, had lived.

One at a time, each man and woman would tease apart the last five days of their son or daughter's grandparent's life in careful detail and describe the gala ceremony on the eve of death that their whole life had been a preparation for. And, as though preparing for the last five days of his or her own life each listener was immersed in divine contemplation.

Among the powerful cords of feeling that tightened their courage and love of life was the knowledge that some day, years hence, their own children would do as they were doing now: commemorate them and at the same time contemplate their own ending, their own final five days. Special attention was then paid to the men and women whose daughter or son's wife was pregnant. A few such cases came to light during every hunting season. They were given the honor of being last to narrate.

The hunting continued until enough meat and hides to trade or work during the coming year had been taken in, usually before the river froze over completely, before the snow was too deep for the wagons to get back. The return journey to the Fjord took twice as long, sometimes two weeks, down the gradual slope of the river plain. Wolves, and bears late to hibernate, approached the mobile camps then, aroused by the stab of hunger and the smell of surplus. Everybody was quiet on the journey back to their permanent home and to the mild land they were reluctantly beginning to farm, dormant for now beneath the snow.

What would they make of me, my father's people, saying all of this to no one in particular, to no one? And at my age! Oh, for a pair of rectangular grey eyes with bony nose and brow to look back at me, worthy of my defiance. Clear away all this doe-eyed shallow-featured softness and love-licking! Show me an icicle! Cut me an icicle. Cut me up into icicles again. Pen the mosquito, release the wolf and the bear; the snow leopard too. Loose them on me and see what they do, see what they make of me. They will give us all the answers we need. Those people do not fuck around with threats or landmines or chemicals or glass eyes or hot baths or roasted swans. None of that. Just BANG! They do. Just do. And what they do they finish. You see? Do and then finish. Do. Finish. Simple. Simple people. Alien.

TWENTY TWO

'I am better than Stan Platt, better than Gerry, better than Brophy, better than Devlin…' Eoin goes through the list, some he had thought were forgotten. They crowd his mind with clean faces.

'Every one of them would be dead by now if they were me,' he thinks. He is, somehow, out in front by his own reckoning. As sure as he can see each once familiar face, as harmless as a brightly painted marionette, he also sees, projected onto a paper screen, his own fierce silhouette, with all the prettiness that color brings to a portrait, and all the detail too, hidden in shadow. He begins to see, too, in large scale, his earlier self with the color and detail that fear and longing had designed still intact, and separate. A cast of characters move and collide at the surface of his thoughts in a swarm that goes all around this still-dark outline he is now becoming.

An immense courage against, not to mention desire for, great calamity tantalizes his imagination, and in turn feeds a fearless appetite in a self-sustaining circuit. Pristine East Germans, spurned Yugoslavians, rutted Turks and all the rest: he could out-shock any one of them. He had more courage in one eye, could focus more purpose in one finger, than they with their entire living beings, than any of their people. Only an army stood a chance against him.

The steering wheel shrinks and creaks in his grip. His mind leaps to build up momentum and then soars off the ramp of fear into oblivious freefall and the sour smell of flocculent spittle on his face returns in his memory to an unexpected welcome.

Eoin sees the spitting snake he had pinned on the mistress's green carpet with his fourteen year old knees. Done nothing but pin it down for a short while, despite the spitting. He had not killed it like it dared him to. He knew it had been a test. A test! Who can understand that? How can that be explained, categorized? How would one categorize what is happening now? To the spitting snake he had shown mercy, allowed it to live when it had wanted to be killed, not believing how easily that could have been arranged. But it could have been. It should have been. It would have been now.

Through the rear mirror Eoin eyes the pile of gear, his material world, trailing a few feet behind him toward the equator at a pace that has no significance because there is no deadline. He pays scant attention to the speed of his Volkswagen, drives slowly enough to keep the car benign and undemanding. He may as well be flying, or not moving at all. He may as well be in Wanderley Wagon.

The mistress had known Eugene Lambert. They might have had common ancestors. Lambert would regularly send her tickets for his show in the mail. She and Eoin would sit together in the Dublin Puppet Theater, a magical place, with the theater lights and soundproofing drawing them into the world of cloth-eared judge and sneaky snake inside Wanderly Wagon. Between Eoin and a small picket fence that marked the boundary of the stage, low-slung head shadows, like his, sat rapt. The mistress would put her arm around him, but each time he would initially resent the distraction before realizing this was part of her enjoyment and how pleasant, in fact, it felt, and how grateful he was to her for bringing him here. But it grew too much for him to receive. His body wasn't used to receiving on this scale. Then a moment of panic about time would come over him, and he would try to gauge how much of it was left. The realization that he would not be prepared for the ending, for what returns were to follow it, upset him too for an additional moment. But it would pass, and he would forget about time and become lost again in its dense thicket, immersed in panic-hemmed joy.

Whenever she laughed and made her truffle-rich sound, and put a hand to her mouth, if she had used her hand around his shoulders the mistress would return it by isolating a lock of hair at his temple and with her nimble thumb and fingertips comb it over the saddle of his ear, as if in compensation for the momentary neglect. He would think, then, that he could start all over again, something that would last.

*   *   *

Day after African day it rained, staving off the inevitable. Storm winds raised the men's oozing clothing, sometimes even their bodies, upwards, upwards then turned with a snap downwards, sideways. The scant mountain verdure screamed to be left alone or else scoured away for good, never to have this done to it again. But neither wish was granted. Only the old boulders bore the turmoil with dumb poise. Lashes of wind were as slaps to the men's exposed faces, the water drops as fat and material as small eggs, until the shells broke against hunger-thinned skin in stings of surprise. It was not jagged or spectacular or even particularly high up there (compared to other mountains in the world) to move one's secret courage. But there were views when the clouds shifted, down as well as out and across, to similar mountains that were higher but looked smaller by some trick of perspective. The other mountains repeated monotonously to eyesight's end.

Those views, when unveiled, had the curious ability to lull one's fear if it grew too sickening, or incite it if it became too mild. I knew from the faces around me that the broken glimpses of scenery had a normalizing effect upon the men who waited for the feared moment to arrive. They had that to be thankful to their god or lucky stars for.

When that moment finally arrived, it would come with instructions on how to cope attached. Until then, waiting. Jap included. Waiting with the de-thighed Napoleon. Napoleon, too, had a stabilizing effect on the swings of fear. It was his quiet endurance of what would perhaps happen to each one of us, soon, prepared or not, that was significant. The state they thought they feared did not look, in reality, as fearful as it felt at its keenest. That is what they were each grappling with, I suspected: the parallax of their imaginations. Perhaps Napoleon's corpse, more than the scenery, kept them doubting, a few envying (who could say, now?) and thinking and debating, and that kept them going, the way that temporary insanity—if they could be considered sane at other times—held them together after dark when they saw nothing, or near to nothing but silhouettes and murk, and their eyes were no match for their ears, their memories and their imagination's creations. But who can know for sure in what way each man drew from the Corsican's corpse his own cushion of comfort?

It made me laugh to think of it. If only you had known me then! If you knew the comfort I could find in places that were not designed to comfort, not even with indifference for comfort, but in places designed to eliminate all traces of human comfort you would call me an extremophile, a mesquite, a protozoan that lives on the unwiped track of swordblood in the uppermost reaches of the scabbard. And you would know the comfort I drew from those men, those brave men, driven like the last and cleverest of sheep, into the same fold the stupid entered first. Would you have thought it possible to sing with so much going on, or threatening to go on, around you? I am not a bad singer, you know. Might you have burst into laughter too? Not insane laughter, but does it matter what kind? I tell you both was easy for me.

TWENTY THREE

After her bath on the night of the visit from Eoin's father the mistress briefly went berserk after dropping a clay ashtray, making her own contribution to the damage. Precious items were then deliberately smashed including, by the pointed toe of a flung Western boot, the lens of the projector that had been left on the floor out of its case with the cap off. They could easily get another one, was not what the mistress wished to hear from Eoin. It only added to her frustration. He knew then, wholly, what he had always instinctively known but had no evidence of before her eruption: that it was wrong to assume he could placate her by speaking. Yet she wanted him to speak, to say things that would placate her, strengthen her up, for she was so weak she trembled and fretted. For what, he could not say for sure. For certain words, but what words? The risks were great. Wrong words (there were so many) might finish her off and, he realized, he had no reliable guide toward the right ones.

Do you think he laughed amid her breakdown? Do you think he found something ticklish in this impossible confusion that suddenly pressed against him? I will let you decide. It does not really matter; the mistress was already mocked by his thoughtful silence. Nothing could have hurt her more than that silence except wrong words, the very thing she desired from him.

In pieces. Like the inanimate objects that could easily be replaced.

She was in pieces. 'Where does it hurt? Where abouts?' He did not need to ask out loud to have the answer. It looped internally: everywhere.

Finally, from among the pain, there came this smile. The smile—of course, it was the slightest of smiles—he discerned, was one she had never worn in his presence before. It was the only thing about her that properly frightened him. Although it did not reveal its meaning in simple to understand words at the time, it made itself known by simpler, more direct means that were purely felt, to be translated into words in the fullness of time, and perhaps written about with embellishment for effect. It was acknowledgement of, and resignation to, a certain type of man. The worthless man. And his line.

It signaled the end of a particular course of action, enough data had been gathered to make one hope-sapping and glaring conclusion, validation of a prejudice that one had temporarily succeeded in overpowering. But to what avail? There was satisfaction (small yet some all the same) in knowing something by the only acceptable, if torturous, means with which the moral mind will allow one to be in possession of knowledge. Even if it is knowledge that you had been wrong. Or, rather, that you had been right, your instinct right, but your unheeding actions wrong. Your prejudices had been right. Caught in error but now it is over and done with and a lesson has been learned. 'Remember to put this knowledge to use in future. Don't be stupid again.' What a bastard to find that out.

Among the minor carnage the sheet of paper was unscathed. She read it without allowing any part of it to touch her. Eoin picked it up off the table and held it for her. Only once did she go back to it, asking him to unfold it for her to re-read it, to set her off again:

'I suppose you . . .don't you understand?. . .how easily this can happen. . . I triple. . .Oh!! It's so easy, Eoin, for them to get to you. . .They are sick you know, they are all sick, all sick! If I could put every one of them in jail for life I would do it. Do you know what they think about piano? The. . .the time. . .the time I went to get you. . . Oh what does it matter now what I tell you?'

So she sputtered bits of ideas, accepting each one's futility as soon as the first words reached her own ears. Yet perhaps her appearance of defeat marked, like a symptom, the beginning of a new wave of relief sweeping over her that was determined to have its day, now, at last.

A framed art-deco poster for the *Trophée Lancôme* hung behind Eoin. A young man twisted neatly at the conclusion of a swing watching his ball arcing toward a far away flag. The mood of that picture had pleased and agitated her since the moment she first saw it as a child in her parent's house. She had always centered the mystery on the odd arrangement of color. But now she must have realized it was the ball, so familiar to her, centimeters away from the flag but not *at* the flag and never would be *at* the flag unless she continued to put it there in her mind, each time she saw the young man's attitude. The picture had drained her slightly but relentlessly. The ball, after all these years, had not moved any nearer to its target. And it never would despite her fantasy because it was not able to move. She could have destroyed it then for deceiving her but for the fact that it was nonetheless one of her cherished possessions. It was French, and now, so easy to understand, more dear than it had ever been, even if she no longer enjoyed it. It was more treasured than this silent boy about whom, along with each new idea that entered her mind, definitive sharp-edged distinctions were being formed, un-resisted.

TWENTY FOUR

One moment (it can last up to half an hour) Eoin sees a terracotta everlasting future. The next moment it vanishes. It is triggered by something he sees far ahead or off to the side of the road, in the cleft of faraway hills: a mosaic of roofs, an orange- or red-capped town emerging from a forest before giving way to a grey and glass city or more forest or rectilinear farmland. The urge to stop never leaves him but until night's approach he does not stop. He keeps driving and watching and listening. Listening to the engine for wear.

A pleasant vacuum pulls his tongue when he sucks air from his bad tooth, followed by a taste of wet bread that is by now familiar. It is something small for him to explore at will before he loses it to a dentist in Berlin. This latest misinformation he dictates to the tape recorder outside the *Statgarten* in Karlsruhe, a place he has never heard of before, as the evening's streetlights are beginning to glow, dimly at first, like hardy night flowers.

He has no business in Karlsruhe, strictly speaking. He is a wayfarer passing through *en route* to another place, and that other place is nobody's concern but Eoin's. Yet the most immediate fact of this town, like most towns, is that it is home to a number of people, and to the dogs they keep.

To comport himself he sets about imagining living in this town, leaving a tooth here. He will pat dogs' heads, if he has to. No fear of rabies: he has a gun that could stop a lion.

The one for dogs that his father once made in the back shed, from a pen, was much smaller, a .22 caliber. It had never failed his father on any breed. It had been on a similar day to this one, around dusk too, when Eoin looked out into the back garden from the chair he was standing on and saw the wooden shed-door at last fly open. Rolling the sly barrel across his fingers with a thumb, his father called him out of the house. He had not allowed his son to see what he was making until it was finished. The Bear Necessities sung by Baloo, floating on his back, had been going round in Eoin's head all day from the previous evening. He had left the cinema as Mowgli, adaptable to any place, believing he would always have a friend, that there was good in everything, even in snakes; at least they were not as bad as he had thought although he still searched for them under and behind the toilet bowl and at the bottom of his bed at night, and still worried that he had missed one hiding somewhere out of sight. Yes, that day he had been able to find good in everything and, behold, the pen-gun for dangerous dogs was a marvelous invention.

'The hostel is full. I am sorry,' says the giggling receptionist the second time he approaches the reception desk, after she gets him to go back and close the door tightly to keep out the Rhenish draft the first time. Is she laughing at him, at the fix she now knows he is in?

'There is another one. . .over. . .(the giggling hampers her) over there. . .(her face reddens). . .with rooms. Her circling finger lands on a laminated map. She breaks into open laughter and turns her head, somewhat slovenly, over one shoulder and speaks in German to the two seated near her. To get to the bottom of this or to leave quickly is Eoin's latest dilemma.

'How far?' he asks her, trying to cut across the joke that might not be on him after all. Her small square teeth chatter in the act of suppressing more laughter; but maybe it is from the draft he has let in.

'Two kilometers,' she splutters.

Wouldn't a glimpse of a gun resolve the mystery? Make her chatter harder but with fear, blameless chattering at least. 'How to reach it?' and, 'Where exactly?' are his final invitations for more humiliating laughter. It is more than he can bear. He stares at this skinny fur-collared woman and slowly withdraws the pistol by the barrel. Smiling himself now, he re-grips and points it at her, extending his arm to steady the aim. He moves it along a deliberate axis from her forehead to her breastbone, back up to her throat, higher again to the T of her nose, then a short line from left to right to cover each spectacle lens. This entire performance he does in his mind but it has the same effect as the act itself. The laughter, and the nonsense he does not understand stops.

He leaves the full hostel feeling he has made an impression, and walks off with his dignity and hope for the future intact once more.

'Spare change?' they used to say in Dublin in those days. They probably still do. It has a simple and lingering ring to it. Beggars had their sayings in immediate post-unification Germany too, that Eoin would later come to understand, but not at this time when it mattered a damn, when it had the chance of mattering. His German is still terrible.

An exploding bullet generally makes a tremendous sound. It is best recognized from some distance where the ears are not overwhelmed by instant, partial deafness, and one can distinguish the wallop from the more prolonged and resonant crack that emerges. Up close it could be any sort of explosion. They have Alsatians in Karslruhe. At least they are the size of allers and their withers slope accordingly to the hips. But most of the dogs have the mangy and mottled coloration of hyenas. He finds himself looking for one with a consistent skirt of golden belly-hair that only the solid black allers lacked. And there seems to be solid black allers too. Fires too. Bonfires lit by men with bandaged arms and beards. Some of the men have shaven heads.

'You shouldn't have been there,' Aaron would probably say before collapsing, in laughter, wishing he were there to see what was about to happen.

'Be brave.' His father speaking again, 'But never show too much bravery, son. It could provoke someone whose reputation depends on appearing braver than you, and they'll make trouble for you. Never be cocky.'

The Karlsruhe dogs are lean but healthy, judging from their shiny teeth. A fire on one side of the stone-paved street hides whatever lies beyond in shadow, a place from where the men and dogs emerge and enter for some mysterious purpose. Occasionally a band of silhouettes shifts *en masse*, perhaps to avoid a thrown blade, if you have a fanciful imagination like Eoin, then regroups in the arc of firelight. He sees mouths open like the beaks of squawking half-birds, Garudas.

As he moves along the street it becomes apparent that these people and their dogs live in this urban campground. What solitary buildings there are, are windowless or have the windows punched out. No lights shine from within. A pistol shot here could have unusual consequences. Eoin tries to predict them.

The problem with carrying a gun is that it sticks its nose into everything. It is a tyrant. After all, if you are not prepared to use it why carry it? the wise saying goes; and if you are prepared to use it, you are ever prepared to use it. If you know guns then you now that they call out constantly for attention, grind down your patience until you must fire at least one round for relief. Devlin would have learned that from Brophy. As a rule, neither of them went around armed. They were the type to come back again later. That was how their minds reasoned. Always cocky about having a later, the dogs that they were. 'What was the point of doubting?' they would say. Eoin would take this Teutonic tribe over Brophy and his people any day because he could tell just by looking at them that their harm was finite, there was some care at their core. Even if they tried to kill him it would not change that standing, it would confirm it. He would do the very same in their boots, defend

openly, not send somebody sneaking after him for days and weeks until.
. .Eoin interrupts his own thoughts.

'When I fire I will stop Devlin first, then Brophy, if he is with him.
Nobody else. Not another person. Never another person again.'

There is always a fat one in films, and maybe that is unfair to the
truth as well as to the fat. But, I swear, in Eoin's case the one that
approaches him is conspicuously over nourished. With an amble too
benign for the threat they both know Eoin poses, he seems to be
dressed like a man that, suddenly disturbed, has hastily risen from under
a pile of garments. Yet who is to say there is not, beneath the tatters he
wears, some aesthetic sensibility in delicate equipoise? Eoin, against all
likelihood, is willing to give him the benefit of the doubt.

'Your dog (a dog walked to heel at his splayed foot) is a *fuchs*,' Eoin is
saying to himself. No: 'your hyena is a *fuchs*.' And he begins to laugh.
But then the fat bastard, if he does not do something with his hands or
arms, some abrupt flutter that instantly recalls Devlin, as though the
wirer himself were approaching. There could have been an image of a
friendly game of darts lying on the near side of that gesture, now lost
forever.

As Eoin involuntarily empties his stomach he remembers, not so
long ago, Yypres and the burdock and the tiny gleaming potatoes that
had nourished him through his sickness, and that brought him to Rush
at early evening with the white-bellied leverets; at last to the indigo rain
clouds, the sparrows, his mother's 'grand. I'm grand here', with it sore
everywhere she touched, to make sure for him.

The barrel knocks against his collarbone when he straightens up
from the splash. Yypres and Rush are gone but he can still see his
mother through the living room window, as he comes back from the
kitchen with the soup for her, crawling to vomit in the far corner of the
garden. The sparrows are pecking at it when he goes out to her, by then
lying on her back away from the indigestible material and the sparrows,
telling him she is grand.

From some distance off the German speaks to him. It does not sound like 'spare change?' Eoin does not understand it. After a gap of silence he speaks to the dog that had barked at the previous utterance. In fright perhaps, or so it seems, the dog whimpers then back-treads.

'Tell him something and see what happens,' Eoin thinks. 'Don't be a tulip! Tell him something. Tell him something about you, on behalf of your people, choose words that are worthy of betokening your life to this man, that will help to account for the debt your presence has run up in his province.'

Tongue-tied is not always a condition of stupidity, if it ever is, but can be symptomatic of an overwhelming *aperçu*. The next morning the fires would be doused, and the camp sealed up and slumbering. The street would have long-boned business types, and joggers with jobs and solid, German cars from Munich and Bochum and Stuttgart and Wolfsburg with mounted racks for athletic equipment; probably even the police. It would seem like a different place. But Eoin is not able to draw much solace from those thoughts.

Still, stepping up steadily to a confrontation is better than certain things he can think of. At least there is a chance, up to the last moment, of avoiding violence. The dog might run away.

The owner is growing less sure of himself the closer they come, his arm movements are on the increase. Yet Eoin also knows that if this goes badly, by conventional standards, all of his problems will be taken care of at once.

A canister explodes in a fire leaving a drawn-out wail. The dog never flinches. He is not gunshy then, a good dog, only pays attention to his master's command. It is probably butane or an air freshener, but it belongs to the same class as riot gas when it comes to the instincts. Each of Eoin's steps seems to grow lighter, as though he is slowly levitating and each muscle in his body announces, separately, its readiness to fly when it is time for the whole to go into action. The sinews in his legs tighten and then relax slightly. The same in his fingers, his neck and back. The effect is to pump him up and the sense of his body switching over to an automatic mode fills him to overflowing with luxurious courage. Or perhaps it is resignation, if there is a difference.

What really matters is that he recognizes it as a familiar state. He relishes the familiar just then, all the more for its pledge to immortality. Ha ha! He can laugh again, close enough to make out the seagull feather dangling from the German's ear and the electric wand that sparkles when he leans down to speak to his *fuchs* again, privately this time, as though rigging a surprise. My good-on-the-outside man! The dog makes its frantic nail-scratching on cue and then takes off and accelerates until the hollow-point removes its face and it tumbles over and over again one more time and then stops moving altogether.

A pause then to fathom the speed at which the last event has occurred and to ask whether everyone has grasped it completely, to allow one to re-assess one's bravery, and to compare it with everyone else's before the next event, whatever event that might be, transpires. Damage to more livestock, to humans.

'*Mensch!*' exclaims Eoin's new occupying voice loudly.

Another funny thing Eoin confirms to be true: everybody is afraid of a solitary gun. Two, three, four guns. . . gradually less fearful. A cache is positively re-assuring. That these men have no guns, then, is instantly clear. The report from the pistol does not do Eoin's safe passage past the camp any harm either. Again, deep down Eoin thinks that these people are basically good. They fear death, respect life, and know what guns can do. They are like a breath of fresh air. It is encouraging. Only a dog has been lost and it has felt not a thing.

From one of the fires another canister explodes as Eoin reaches the end of the street. Behind him, the camp and its inhabitants, and now the shell casing, are still growing as notions in his mind but much, much too slowly to worry about. He does not look behind him. His ears are ringing. He knows what has made the last noise. He knows that if he has to, he can live in karley surley.

TWENTY FIVE

In the early 1600s, while the world was in ferment, currents of air rose up from countless yellow candle-flames in silence. They still do.

When I stare at and into a candle-flame until it demurs, and sashays, and its tip hurries to scatter hot air like seed, I demure too. If then a wind comes, even the faintest shift in air pressure, and the flame leans back too far, panics, and produces pips of grey smoke, I give a little panic too and look for the source of the wind. When it passes I feel better. I then pay more attention to the curvature of the flame, and notice how, after a spell of guttering, it is less responsive, almost unresponsive, to my gaze. It appears not to move and I have to rely on my memory to know that subtle movement is always taking place. I have to assume things.

Have you ever watched a candle flame that did not move? It is exciting because you do not believe your eyes. You tell yourself it is moving, that you just cannot detect movement. You defer to your knowledge. Anyway, you tell yourself, it will not last—this apparent stillness—because there are too many drafts around. So you enter a state of anticipation, which equates with excitement. Putting that aside for a moment you will, if you concentrate, observe that the still flame is more a carving knife than a dagger. One side is straighter, on account of the unavoidable curling of the wick. You wish the tip were sharper to make it a better knife but it is blunt until it is suddenly needle-fine and then you are vindicated, secondarily, in your faith that it has been moving after all. The movement was all in the tip. You were right all along. But you had been looking at the whole flame, especially the tall bright arch of the center, when you struggled with disbelief at its apparent stillness. Now you know the trick, so you focus on the dimmer tip from now on and forget about the rest until the next wind comes along. You watch the end of the flame and you think—forsaking knives for a moment—that it resembles a yellow felt-tipped pen that has been used to write words on blue-lined notepaper.

Eoin burns candle after candle for no good reason, except to see each one burn down and, at a surprise and precise moment, irrevocably go out. A series of suns, or of sunlit days, he thinks, all the while feeling a figure creep up on him, tough and wolfish, heckle just out of reach (but not by much) and then slink away again when he considers turning to look.

The centuries are more in Germany. Everywhere one sees earth-marks made upon older earth-marks, laid under the ageless sun and the fresh sky. The tiredness of the centuries, and the countless bodies that bore it, and continue to bear it, is easy for Eoin to sense in this place.

The crust of the present is thinner than each of us is capable of fully knowing, is prepared to realize; all this could not have turned out, be turning out this way, otherwise. And the future is recklessly deceiving each one of us. But the past is here before our eyes, not only in Germany, just especially so. Here it all is. The heaving and puffing to reach exhaustion immortal, dispossessed from the short-lived bodies, candle after candle, flame, ember, smoke, ash. The nature of the mistake is the hardest thing to grasp. There is simply nothing as big to compare it to. The heat from a sun and the heat from a candle.

One burning candle grows in familiarity to its very end, to where it is thickest and most tired, and when it goes out the new one Eoin lights is much too jaunty, too enthusiastic and unfamiliar at first. But he notices how it inevitably grows on him until he is able to live exclusively within its span of light, with as much awareness as he has ever been able to summon for anything in the present in his life. Chunks of light. Chunks of time. Chunks of life. Present life. He comes to know more and more, to feel enriched.

Every evening Eoin burns candles. Often, too, in his mind when he sleeps at night, and even during certain days, especially when the sun comes out while he digs and hefts, candles burn. It is on one of those sunny days that a steel spike comes over the fence. It skewers a cat as it creeps over a clay camber with a slice of meat trailing from its mouth. As Eoin is examining the diminishing strokes of the cat's limbs an anonymous cry of *Mensch!* rings out from the direction of the spear's source. A second spear strikes the ground Eoin had been impressing with his footprints only a moment before. The ground yields with a grating sound that is cut short by the next punch of the giant pile-hammer, also on the far side of the fence. Eoin puts out a cry of his own. That cry goes up against and is drowned by the hammer too.

The fence is high and long. Eoin has no time to visit the other side to make enquiries. A Turk he sees every day, working on the same side, notices Eoin's startle and hears the *Mensch!* and watches the cat expire. But when the third spike fails to materialize he carries on working as though nothing has happened. Perhaps Eoin's shout has been enough after all, has been heard by the unseen thrower, as Eoin has heard the *Mensch!* between the beats of the pile-driver. Yet for all he knows the machine is releasing a continuous volley of steel splinters with every blow and the two he saw have merely flown astray. Perhaps, on the other side of that fence, dead cats and men lie twitching together in pop-eyed surprise, to be cleared away and buried at day's end when the air will resound with the silence that returns after the hammering stops. The one who cried *Mensch!* is the last to have held out, for all he knows. He hears nothing more but the incessant wallop and shivering ring.

Shaken, he sees himself as if from outside, as somebody who is shaken, from a vantage with a vast perspective on his tiny position. But who is he, the one who is looking at himself? He remembers his mother's words and tries to find some help in them, even if only in her tone of expression: 'You are a special boy. There is nothing you cannot do.' But there is nothing he can do. They are dead words, meaningless, mean. He sees her hot eyes that never lie, growing impatient now, impatient after waiting all this time for him to prove what she had prophesied is true, to act upon what he believes, and not just what is laid out before his eyes at the present moment. To act upon what he knows.

He believes nothing. He knows nothing.

TWENTY SIX

Here is what another person might have realized quicker: the mistress could be close to only those who resembled, to her, herself; people she decided had had a similar type of life. Those were the ones she would bathe in attention. Each morning she awoke to a slightly greater strain. An elastic band, already taut, had to be stretched a little more and thus there was a sense, in her way of living, of a double burden: maintaining the current tension without backsliding, and adding to it.

How could she have had so little self-regard? Whatever she accomplished for herself in this foreign country where she had chosen to live, as far as garnering admiration went, was worthless to her. It certainly was not enough, by her measure, to motivate her to perform the minor acts of day-to-day living. On top of that the idea of any recognition being accorded, through her actions, to her people, about whom it is almost certain nobody but Eoin knew very much, was abhorrent. If anything it was an added impediment to her motivation. She believed and accepted, she wrote, in English, in the diary she kept conspicuously open on top of the piano, that her life was 'a spark spat from a fire. . . spectacular and interesting but without an important destiny. And just like a spark, previously non-existent within the fire. . . unidentifiable. Outside of the fire, I carry a threat to all that is flammable. . . that might come into contact with me and burst into and be consumed by my fire.'

She wanted to start something of her own, she wrote more directly on another occasion. But what else could a spark start but a fire? 'I must do my bit toward putting an end to my line. . . but even more. . . every act I consciously commit must try to undo what my line has already done.' To do that, though, she must have known that she had recourse only to the tendencies and inclinations that, however finely differentiated she tried to perceive them in herself, were, if truly hers then *ipso facto* indisputably of her line and no other. They were suspect from the outset and not to be trusted until after the act when, measuring the results, any merit could be retrospectively apportioned.

And she needed results. She needed to know one way or another, preferably as fast as possible, whether she had done something good or bad, if she was capable of good or if only of bad. Her reactions were anger if the result was bad, sadness if it was good. But in the good she would often later find bad under a colder eye, and frustration where she could not decide. If you had asked her which she preferred, she probably would have said to do good. But bad was probably better in practice because, strange to say, it made it easier to stretch out another day and carry on trying.

It seemed she was after a result from her actions so great that it would be terminally reassuring, unnecessary to go on stretching any longer; or an especially bad result to give her enough anger to snap her elastic life. Strung so tightly it threatened to snap each day and would not.

Without fresh results there was nothing. But any thoughtless act by somebody with so much potential for conflagration (by her own self-appraisal) was surely frightening to conceive of. That was the daily tension. Every inclination, even the most trivial, had to be intercepted and re-circuited toward the massive effort to redress something of the past, turn it into manure for fragile seedlings.

Later that important night, and calm again though it was not easy for her, the mistress told Eoin that her own father had gone off many times alone into the desert. He was searching for the fennec fox. He had told her and nobody else because, he said, nobody would believe him. He wanted to find a pup and send it back to her in France. The ones sold in the towns, in cages, had been mistreated by the Arabs, and made bad pets, he told her. He was going to find her a healthy one.

He went by bicycle, using routes he had driven along on his patrols during the day, with a basket tied to the back. The desert glows in the dark, he assured her, it was easy to find the way. Up in the sky there must have been stars to beat the band.

'How, Papa? How are you going to catch the fox?' she had asked him.

'With a torch my dear. I will tell you, if you will be patient.'

She had willed herself to be patient. The bicycle was quiet but it had no lights for picking up the animals' eyes, so he carried a torch in the basket. Sometimes he would cycle all through the night, walking where the road had been bombed—lifting the bicycle over the craters—or blocked with wrecked vehicles, cadavers.

'Weren't you afraid, Papa, of the Arabs and their bombs?'

When she asked this question he grinned like an overachieving liar. But he was not lying about the facts he gave to her. That, at least, could be said of him, she told Eoin, without further explanation.

It had been so hard to find a good fennec fox. He had seen many, found the lairs and handled the pups while their mother circled outside, but could not find any good enough to send back except for one. On the night in question he had fallen from his bicycle and the wheel was so warped it would no longer make a full turn. As he fell to the ground he disturbed a fennec bitch that had been crouched in the hope he would continue on his way and leave her unmolested. She had been taking meat from a soldier a few steps away. The soldier's motorcycle lay on its side, down below in the dry riverbed like a horse trying to get up.

He followed the desert fox with the torch and saw it enter a space on a jagged crest of rock. As he climbed up carefully, he began to hear the young mewling inside. He stopped to listen for a while. He tried to make out how many there were. Through the harsh arid air came a fading smell of new life from the small cave. A smell of damp soil, of spring rain.

It was a smell, he said, that reminded him of his youth in Passy, and the garden his mother had loved. It was easy for the mistress to remember this detail because it was the first time her father had mentioned his mother to her without bitterness, and it seemed inexplicably dishonest. In fact it cast a dishonest veil upon the entire story. It drew a feeling from her that was like being enjoined to revive a long-withered flower.

He waited, concealed by a fin of rock, until the bitch's huge ears re-appeared in silhouette, swiveled against the ultramarine sky, and she had dropped down in her practiced way, front legs together like a lady, to the flat riverbed and returned to the carrion. He went to the mouth of the cave and switched on the torch, filled with excitement.

As the mistress told the story of her father's quest for a good fennec fox in the Algerian desert, a new tone in her voice struck Eoin's ears. In it he found something labile, resembling the type that his own father had alleged her to be ('the type she really is') a few hours earlier. Everything she said, from that point on, he seemed to automatically treat with caution, triangulated between his father's description of her and his own slipping memory of her prior character. It was an exhausting process. It must have been some degree of heartlessness that the mistress sensed in his attitude that drove her on so, perhaps in an attempt to melt some of the understanding that had welled up between them during the past seven years, now inexplicably frozen. Perhaps she was proving her love by revealing, however insignificant the details might be to anyone else, secrets that were of the greatest value to her. Maybe she hoped that he might volunteer the high-worth details of his own experiences, to ground her inklings about those details, and to set them up alongside her own, bring it all out once and for all.

Dicey, it was nevertheless her chance to finally procure a stable and satisfying companion beyond the realm of fantasy.

Still, who is to say that any of what she said that night was true at all and not an elaborate scheme? Eoin's father would have seen through any play in an instant. He would have known. Eoin himself was not sure, and though he could not listen entirely sympathetically he made a sincere enough effort to out of habit. She had said so much, smoked so much, and stared over his head so much. It seemed like talking to Eoin and smoking were to be the last important deeds of her life, the last deeds of all. Every ounce of concentration she could muster went into both. It seemed it would be endless too, all routine activities indefinitely suspended. It was as if everything were on the verge of falling into its proper category of importance at long last.

Inside the cave, she continued, a single pair of reflecting eyes and a bar of ears like cowhorns stuck out from the solitary, curled creature that was visible behind a lip of stone that gave the lair a *chic* design. Mixed with the various bones that lay around was probably, her father said, the remains of a brother or sister that had not had the strength to survive.

TWENTY SEVEN

The samples of living I have seen and said yes to without hesitation. How can I account for them? What made me so sure that in giving up time, then, I would have it back later, even when I began to split into confused fragments, once taking a shower while putting on my clothes to save time, and going to extraordinary lengths to keep them dry. And when I gave up trying to keep my clothes dry and resorted to masturbation but could not stiffen, but also could not get it out of my mind, and could not speak because there was no time to lose but still so much I needed to do because I was so far behind.

One problem for me, I later discovered, was never telling anybody my idea. The mistress had been Eoin's best chance to tell his. After her it was too complicated for him to tell another. I found that out when I tried, too, and I had no choice but to keep the idea to myself. Yes, I admit now, it would have been like talking to them in a foreign language they did not know or care to learn. I could have probably tried to break my idea down into bits but that was too difficult, and too easy to fuck up, knowing how people tend to construe with lunch or dinner just around the corner. Or afterwards with their stomachs full.

I was waiting and waiting until I had the whole idea arranged tightly and neatly and completely. Then I was going to present it to everybody and show them all what I had been working on in secret. I would leave them gasping at my idea, turning their own ideas on end. I would have them reconsidering all that they thought they knew. That was the work that I had to do, alone. They would be able to see why it had to be done this way, and they would understand how certain things could happen. Ways by which animals had to die.

With My gone, my skin is gone. I am down to an oozing subcutaneum. At least I finally know a little more about Jap. The chafe of the dense and salted sea level air is enough to sting my entire exposed body. The scraping of present life against my worn and resistant carapace offers no let up, accepts no excuses, is deaf to my story. It is in constant tension to tell its own story *to me* before my time is past. I understand it. I shall go on unloving it, though, like all that is willful, insistent.

I cannot remember how many days it is since she left. I used to measure days by seawater showers because that is where I could still combine the sight of the white-sailed squall-craft, white as a virgin, with the smell of My's bud opening to raspberry around my nose, her open palms wet against my calloused hide. But my hide is electrified now, as if it believes that if raw enough, charged enough, a spark will issue, reaching My in the remote stilt house where some legless bastard no doubt sits near her now. I have not showered in I know not how long. I must smell like Frank. I can no longer smell Frank.

Days I forget or choose not to eat on purpose to stay alive. No I am not kidding. I do not even put my teeth in, let a rapidly-growing lime-green algae film them on the ledge beside me. There is nobody to distract me with puzzling care now. We all know our proper place. All is as it should be. I pay them and they do as I command. Acts of initiative occur no longer. I have learned my lesson.

All the better for them if I get malaria, out on the night strand, like a shipwrecked tar waiting to be removed from this Tír na nÓg. I have paid up a year in advance. They can scoff all they like. I am eating little because it helps me concentrate, jogs my memory like nothing else I know. I may not leave this alien paradise but my story has a chance, a version of it that I will hack into completion if necessary. If only to save your blessed life, my dear, who has stayed with me so long, full of poison from my own hand, who deserves to recover and to live long. You I am determined to save. You I still love!

*　　*　　*

The fennec pup was perfect. When he lay down the torch, aimed the beam away to the side of the cave and reached his hand out, she came to him bravely, to the smell of the bloody scratches on his hands. It was as though, he told her, this animal that had never known humans was unafraid of them. He had never seen one quite like it in the wild. The tiny tongue licked and the soft teeth nipped the thigh of his thumb.

He knew the fox would be a good pet but it was a long walk back to the garrison and if he was not back before daybreak, and shot by a sniper, the fennec would die too. Alone, without the basket, he could have taken a more direct route over the escarpment and easily got back while it was still night. But that was impossible with the fox.

When he picked her up he noticed something about one of the eyes, a discoloration, a loss of luster and something around the edge of the lid. Blue mucilage was how he remembered it later but at the time paid it little attention.

During the story the mistress sometimes deviated from the storyline. She had never mentioned her mother to Eoin until now. It was like a matter that could not be put off any longer. Her tired mother whom she said she loved but seemed to despise for doing certain things and not doing others. For cleaning up but not remarking on what had been left in a neat pile on her bedroom floor: a small rick of excrement, drying slowly through the night beside her slippers, while the grown body moaned, naked but for a vest, and her mother remained in the next room until breakfast. She remembered weakly, she said, yet to this day with shame, the hours she had lain awake in the dark, inattentive, failing to recognize the befouling in spite of the overpowering smell and the closeness of her father. In spite of his identifiable voice repeating the baleful mantra that she could not bring herself to repeat to Eoin.

Maybe it was for the sake of some idea of fairness that the mistress split her story like this. Maybe she was afraid of any one item or act having hegemony over others that co-existed but, by chance and the linearity of speech, had not emerged yet from her mouth, had to be queued into sequence. Maybe she had made a rule of thumb some time ago, a promise to herself that when speaking from her heart to keep as close a match as possible between her speech and the running course of her thoughts, to limit the regret afterwards.

Certain words or phrases seemed to trigger a switch that extended to her tone as well. Phrases like 'paid no attention'. Then, when she appeared to run out of words, about to lose the ability to go on with her story, she would come upon a word such as 'spring' and, as though brought out from—or, perhaps more correctly, put under—a hypnotic spell, she would return to her original story revived, her voice stronger. She seemed afraid of what her heart was asking her to say to another person, perhaps because she had always felt its danger to be less if left unsaid and, even more importantly, now realizing how it had molded her.

Strangely, this switching of speech and tone inspired her as if it were a test of her personal strength to remain within the bounds of self-control, and she found herself doing well enough all things considered.

At the same time she must have thought that, to Eoin's ears, what she said, the amplitude of her waves of revelation, was huge. It was not. The waves were small to his ears. There was nothing he could do about that, except listen and try to pity her for her suffering. Or for not having suffered more. Although he felt as wise and alone as a barn owl, he still wanted to hear what happened to the solitary fox cub with its diseased eye. It was that part of the story he wanted to hear. The sugar perhaps.

Her legs were straight. Her thighs tapered to beautiful-boned knees and again her calves were clean downward strokes to the ankles. But it was the way she moved her legs that gave them their powerful draw, the rhythm with which she moved them, pushing them together and extending her toes, drawing them up and closing her ankles, sometimes parting them clam-like in rare unself-conscious moments, but never crossing them, as if never trusting them to repose.

In her manner of smoking and adjusting her legs, now in woolen tights, she resembled, to Eoin, a girl afraid to go home to face her parents. But she did not speak like one. She spoke thoughtfully, more like a judge who has sent murderers to the gallows, set innocents free and is suddenly surprised to find herself puzzled and pre-occupied with why that had been any of her business in the first place. A unanticipated conclusion to an impeccable career.

If you are developing the impression that the mistress was building herself up to some declaration, or else stirring Eoin toward some declaration, or perhaps an ecstatic union of the two (one between the pair of them might have been enough to bring it about), that she felt the crush of time running out before the proper, to her way of thinking, setting had been established for this to happen naturally, ideally, safely, then you will be squarely in Eoin's shoes. Yet she could not betray the story of the Saharan fox. It was the only Braille she had. So she went on with it.

Where was the bread, the ticking range, the warm colors, the turned soil, the potatoes? Had she told him what he was susceptible to, what he sensed, what he had loved about her, might not it all have been different? The dam would surely have burst open, the water purified as it dashed upon dry rock and sluiced through settling, oval pebbles. The love would have separated out from everything else and hurled invincibly along, mile after mile, to the open country, never picking up stagnant growth. They would have fallen together out of their captor's basket, rolled a little down a slope, with some bruising granted, and come to rest under the open sky where they belonged to nobody, free to have their own pleasure. Free to have their own experiences. But how could she have known that? Hard as she tried, the mistress was not living her own life. Not to mention not living Eoin's either.

The television was still on with the volume turned down as she talked and he listened. Nausea hung in the air. Orange CIE trains, endless in perspective, waited in black and white tiled railroad stations somewhere in Ireland. The smell of diesel smoke leaked through the screen. Friendly, twitching heads, the type Eoin would one day see through the windows of Gerry's car, saying things he was unable to hear, but knew would be staggeringly superfluous, mimed on the silent screen.

Sometimes she glanced at those faces on the screen too. But mostly she looked at Eoin, or above him at the *Trophée Lancôme* man, or at his hands, which he allowed her to, not hiding the chamfered last knuckle of his right hand that had become, he intuitively knew, a totem for her of Eoin's first seven years of life. Horror's art. The last object that intact right hand had held was a banister post, one spring night, when Eoin's father swung the home-made steel knife forged in his shed. Eoin would never play a perfect nocturne. But he could now play a good nocturne. By her will.

*   *   *

What am I saying? What am I afraid of not being exquisite enough about, of not knowing enough about, of being presumptuous about? Everything, when it boils down to it. Forgive me this weakness that has become my ruler, my vice. I must be sure to tell you something, even if the certainty is fleeting. I dwell violently on what I do not know like a genius who thinks he is nearing absolute knowledge of the system. That is my brain, restlessly obsessed by what is unknown. Along the way I have learned to digest rock.

I do not expect you to believe me but I have met more extravagant goals, defied greater challenges. It is not to boast, to repair what you might take to be my pride's abandonment, but a dab of color to help you see me as I quite possibly really am. A dab here, a dab there, soon dabs everywhere and bingo!—you see what I am able only to feel! What nonsense.

The fennec fox, before you, before I, curl up and die of shame.

The bladder of watered wine, hooked to his webbing belt, was too small to serve, cut open, as a pouch. The fox might fall out. He would have to use the basket after all. Despite the cold he removed his undershirt to protect the fox inside. As he lowered his open hand the animal sprung off into the chamber and stomped around the bedding before sitting for a moment. Then the front legs collapsed and it lay comfortably. He managed to get down to the riverbed one-handed and thought he saw the mother moving among the rocks, watching him. Then he set off, walking quickly.

At one point along the long trail that cut straight across a great bow of road he had cycled along earlier in the night, he scooped out an inch of cold sand and stone and sat on the warmer under-layer drinking and interpreting the conspiracy of whispers the desert night offered up in support of even one's wildest imaginings.

Out of sight the land teemed with incipient peril, but its crushing beauty became dry of the sentimentality he felt evaporating from the plain surface of his mind. He said it was a case of purification, desiccation, distillation or crystallization. Transformation of energy and matter from one form, one place, to another form and place in a controlled and efficient operation.

A spirit more stimulating than any alcohol ran through and used him for its superior, incomprehensible work while he sat observing the little part that was within his intelligence's purview. The piece of desert life around him held the secret to this strangely intense bond between himself and the world that he was afraid would destroy him if he experienced too much more of it.

Instead of a full surrender he came close enough to imagine one. From there intense feelings flowed by but he held control over them. They were as intense as he allowed them to be, the limit of what he could control, as exhausting as it was exhilarating, and as meaningless to his later memory.

The dim glow of the plain spreading for miles southwards was marked with the oddly-shaped shadows of hills and islands of rock. Out there, beyond the resolution of his eyes, Arab fires and lamps and pipes burned. Camels and horses lay on the ground. Some of the fires he thought he could see, at the corners of his eyes, as silver stars that vanished when he looked directly toward them. It gave him a sense that they were constantly moving, like the adult fox, to avoid observation. He knew that those silver lights piercing the darkness represented people who wanted—and would always want, no matter what he did or who he became—to kill him.

The monotony of meaninglessness and escalation of fear drove him to his feet and he set off again, this time with a more willful attitude against a pity he was certain he felt for the fox that had begun to agitate him. Each step seemed to be killing the animal. As his thoughts began to weigh him down he fought against his pace slackening. Soon he found it impossible to hurry. It took immense effort just to keep moving.

Eoin might well have untied his tongue that night in return for this wonderful story, when there was still time. When there was a possibility she might have accepted more from him, looser things that were likely to be off the mark. What chance had there ever been before the lunch bell rang, even if he had known how to tell her, known precisely what to say? Had he untied his tongue he might have had all those thousand and one nights of his past back again with leverets, and not stouts, to be repeated as long as the future lasted.

'No longer races through the shadows from large-bodied smiles, large hands heavy and dry, and repetitive as pistons, stopping my lungs and whispering inside my head words in familiar voices, but unfamiliar rhythms.'

Could he have said that to the mistress?

"'In this weather," my mother warned, "close all the doors of the house. All of them. Close all the doors to keep out the rain!" But they were so many, and the latches so complicated, and they were so clever! They watched, didn't they, pretending they were busy with other things, and when I went to my room, and she to hers, at night in the wind and rain, they were too quick. They stopped me, they made me let her down and admit I couldn't do what she told me to do. Exactly the thing she told me to! When was she coming back? When would they—the large, fast ones—go away from here so I can close the doors and lock them? But the face! I cannot look at it in the dark, it is too frightening, too clever and sly, the eyes are watching from the corners like a shy friend, too shy to talk to me in their normal way. But they are not shy! They are the opposite of shy! But I can't believe it and you too, wouldn't believe it, so nice they seemed, so far away and occupied. Until then. But he was watching all the time, and waiting for the dark, for the rain, for me to start running. Then he came like a noisy wind and beat me to the locks, to the shutters, and it was always when the lights were not working. And no sleep. No sleep for a thousand and one nights, and a thousand and one more again, waiting for the shy friend to come between my Mama and me, and leave me, before all the rest, waiting for a race I would lose through the dark night that belonged to all the faceless noises that stirred against my movement toward sleep. The race toward a locked and shuttered room where I might sleep safely, and not have to wait for the door to open, and the struggle.'

But the mistress had always started one of her own stories, and Eoin felt bound to listen and put his own aside. Soon he forgot his own. Then the bell would finally ring, and when it came it brought relief.

TWENTY EIGHT

Later that same day, after surviving the steel spikes, Eoin buys thirty meters of cellophane at the *Kaufhalle*. Back at his room in the *Wohnheim* owned by the construction company he wraps his naked body from ankles to neck, doing his arms and face separately, leaving gaps to breathe and see through.

How it came to occur to him to do this he could not say if a gun were put to his head. But it gives him enormous relief to seal every pore. By maneuvering his shrink-wrapped body to the wall mirror, the relief is even greater when the face he sees is unrecognizable, as though someone else has gotten themselves into this preposterous but interesting predicament, and that other is unaware of any duplication, or of being watched.

With the door locked he remains, throughout that long summer evening, lying on the bed. He occasionally moves to the mirror for a few moments to confirm the thoughts running through his mind. It is paradoxically calming to be giving into frightening urges.

The fire that has been constantly scorching his body is doused. The unrelenting panic has relented. His mind, which had seemed blank before, but from this moment seems to have been overloaded, is truly blank now. He seems to be beginning from scratch, beginning to familiarize himself with the strange man in the mirror who appears calm, unthreatening, understandably pathetic.

He sees the room where he has lived for half a year for the first time. It is not pleasant but it is acceptable. As calmness descends he begins to see the problem laying outside of the room, the construction site, Karlsruhe and Germany. It lays outside of all the rest that he thought he had, but had not, up to now, perceived. When he tries to picture what lies outside and his relationship to it he repeatedly thinks of the toddler tripping in Yypres. The path to this room where he is wrapped in cellophane has been so big, he senses, the distances insurmountable by anything but a body, a mindless body. He had set off, initially, faster than his mind could travel and now he has fallen. Yes, that is it, he thinks. That is what has happened.

He finds other eyes when he looks up. All of them—his father's, his mother's, the mistress's—have the same expression. It is expectancy. But that does not matter now because a tremendous heat rises from his throat and his nose and eyes. It carries with it end-of-life tears that are expected to be as damaging as stray bullets in the presence of those other eyes. But this time he cannot help himself and so he says quietly: 'It does not matter'. The words sound simple.

*   *   *

It may have been the querulous tone in Eoin's voice that soothed his father as he made his way to the bedroom, to awaken the boy who was not asleep, and ask him whether he was alright. A cascade of lights going on and off signaled his approach. All but the landing light, which was left on, sending a low volume of light into the bedroom through the glass panel above the door. That and the heaviness of each step. The belt of his trousers already loosened, the buckle's tinkle reached Eoin before it contacted the hollow-paneled door, making a scraping sound. Then a mysterious moment: a pause before the door slowly opened, allowing a little more light in.

His father's voice was now hoarse, and clotted by the mincemeat stew, and the bread with the butter now smeared on his chin that Eoin had heard him eat in the quiet after the shouting and throttling. She had made gurgling cries, his mother. She was lucky to have it behind her now, at least. The hoarse voice made its enquiry: ' Alright, Eoin?'

Y'alright, Eoin?,' then a bit louder: 'Alright, son?'

His mother could surely hear. Or could she? Maybe she was dead. In any case it was just him and his father now.

Behind the wrist of his father's left hand a wad of kitchen paper showed. He seemed to be nursing a wound. Closer to the side of the bed he arrived, in a concerned and thoughtful way, his voice going lower. The question became a statement: 'Alright, son.'

The weight of the other's body tightened the covers and made them a straitjacket. Having his arms pinned led Eoin to think that his greatest panic had been reached, but this was always wrong. When the hand—dry and heavy, heavier than its dead weight would have been, Eoin thought—went across his face as if it were a belly to press, no longer a face requiring the nose or mouth to be free of obstructions in order to breathe, to stay alive, his panic of dying was greatest.

There was nowhere to turn his face but into the pillow or harder against the suffocating, pressing hand. It was up to himself to live or die. He could grab a breath between the slow repetitive strokes and hold it while he was blindfolded and smothered.

The mind is so clever. When required, it can focus all of its power on one simple thing, ignore the rest to keep alive. Eoin read that in a book.

By the time his father opened his buttered lips and allowed them to enfold and involute and to suck against Eoin's tightened mouth, the breath pouring out of his father's nose like puke smoke, and into Eoin's, rattled his stomach walls.

The assurances his father gave him were honest, heartfelt. Over and over he assured him that he loved him, and he would never allow anything to happen to him, would never allow anybody to hurt him, would never hit him. He was a good boy, he told him again and again. He was a good boy. Any attempt to struggle might endanger that.

'You were always a good boy, I never had to lay a finger on you'. 'You are better than any other boy.' 'You are a special boy.' Over and over again.

Eoin saw the slick of melted butter moving over the surface of warm stew after his father dipped his folded slice of bread in. In turn the buttery gravy soaked into the underside of the bread and all pressed against his mouth and chin, bitten with small brown teeth. Some of the waste now clung to Eoin's face. He could feel its chill and smell it. The rancidity made him want to shit. He trembled it away.

Wide-awake, he found a use for those alert moments. A pragmatic boy. He would summon his enemies—the ones outside the room—and convince himself that if this night passed without dying he would never submit to any of them again. It was the one time he could contemplate the worst of his enemies without a trace of fear. That is what he concentrated on: defeating all other enemies, and his promise to exult, the following day and on into the future, in the pacified outside world he would no longer be afraid of.

TWENTY NINE

My's replacement has appeared. The novelty disturbs me. By way of introduction she tells me My is dead. It is to spare my feelings, I was initially prepared to concede, to make me think that she does not know the real reason My did not return. She invents a story about a bus crash, which I refuse to go into, and puts considerable effort into the telling. She even manages to cry.

It makes me instinctively mistrustful. She knows as well as you do that I was not born yesterday. These vertical lines that fence in my skull like the workings of cheese wire would, one might think, have warned her against deceit. It does not and I take note. We will have difficulties, I predict, if I can be bothered. Until then I will let her have her way, let her think she guides what I think, that the familiarity she covets is just beyond the horizon.

That is my immediate plan for Suzu, who I already recognize as Suzi—an aptly inane name for an insensitive drone with notions about people like me, and people like Frank. We are the same people to her. You see the problem, put roughly?

I bet she is capable of eating anything, shits felty pellets, a dozen of them every morning in a single sitting. She could probably drop them on the move if she wished to, no bother. There is something about the way she stands and stares, and makes to move away but hesitates, causing something about her head to sway, her ears maybe, that is goatish. I should know, goatishness runs on my mother's side among the men and some of the women as well, even the orangey flecking of the iris, from what I gathered through the magnifying glass I used on the few color photos that existed, once upon a time, within my ambit.

The thought of Suzi's fingers on my knee sends deep pain, bone pain, flaring right to the hip. Frank is getting along with her, as I expected. It emboldens her toward me. Two against one, she thinks, without knowing anything of the one, the girth of that one. I would cut her into pieces and take her ice fishing. In the deepest frozen fjord lower her gently over the wide waxen lip of the ice hole to an unseen galaxy of mouths far beneath. She has not a clue what I am capable of. I have not yet the desire to search for a way to explain.

'Eeny meeny miney mo, catch a nigger by the toe. If he squeals, let him go. Eeny meeny miney mo,' is what I say to her. But she just gives a little laugh, a snort really, does her goat flinch half way through and, after settling the tray of food down beside me, goes over to Frank with his big snowman's smile and small sneaky teeth, gapped and grey. He can have her.

'How old are you?' I say in Khmer, the next time she passes. My taught me Khmer words.

'Twenty two,' she answers in French, with the bare minimum of effort and her tone is decidedly disdainful.

'*Mille neuf cent quatre vingt...?*' I scavenge for these words so she cannot say them. She probably only knows numbers in French. But she ignores my prompt.

'*Le premier Janvier.*'

I say nothing and time—precious time—passes by.

'At exactly midnight,' she finally adds.

She has enjoyed pushing me. From that I surmise she has brothers, at least one of which has been wounded, or killed, and a father or a mother that is still alive. Of course I will never ask her. I am not really interested. I am just waiting for her to try to touch me. She is lying about her age.

She could be My's sister—a younger sister perhaps. All the same gestures and mannerisms she puts on, minus the authenticity of course. A mere mimic. Frank must have told her about me. She tries to appear enthusiastic. My nerves quiver in response, and I grow squeamish. But I do not attack her. It is not altogether repulsive to draw the interest of a newcomer, however fake it might be. To stop now—I think about it every day since My left me—I would need brakes. I do not have brakes. There is only inertia, and that I have no power over.

*   *   *

In his last BASF cassette tape recording Eoin promises another to follow a week later but it never does. Nobody to blame. Slipping all the time, it finally slips off his list of concerns. The day of the dentist comes at last. Another dentist might have been able to save more of them. It is somewhat comforting though to see this dentist, Wagner, appalled.

Had he only acted sooner, Wagner says. But Eoin is not disconsolate. The cleanliness, the mild, localized raising of pain, the hushed sounds and their lingering echoes, the worn leather chair are all immensely soothing and re-invigorating, divine. Thick smooth skin with two deep-set lines around the mouth above a sculpted beard of tinsel hair makes Wagner's age difficult to gauge. His large-framed glasses make light refractions, like amber, from the edges and corners, while the lenses are mirror and window to Eoin's eyes as he works.

Later, drinking in his room, Eoin approaches an assertive mood that is rare and troubling. He goes outside to find a telephone. If the number had been even one digit longer he might not have completed the dialing, so quickly does his mind begin to clear in the sobering air of the autobahn underpass.

As the phone rings down the line, Eoin spots the Turk who witnessed the cat's impalement. He is approaching in the distance with what looks like a wife and there is a child running ahead of them in the waning evening light. The woman wears a dark headscarf and darker clothes. A flashing crescent of light between her legs below the knees is the only evidence of her walking. Her husband has an exaggerated articulation, bouncing on bowed legs, arms swinging. He is pointing for the child who tries to ignore his father as much as he thinks will be tolerated. The boy looks about five.

At first Eoin doubts what his eyes are telling him. He is used to seeing this man in work clothes. The walk and the shape of the head are familiar, but his leather jacket, white shoes, and his combed and oiled hair is conspicuously a part of some large world. It is an idea, Eoin realizes, that he had not considered before. He had not placed the Turk in any world.

By the time the man's face and voice become unmistakable, a girl has answered the phone, a Mancunian girl. She is not Claire or Aaron, and does not know them. She confirms the number, and finds no stupidity in asking whether Eoin has a forwarding address for some mail that looks important, from Germany it seems. At least it saves him the trouble of asking her the same question. The Turkish couple are upon him and the boy is well past and making gunfire sounds as Eoin thinks of something to say to the stranger in England besides goodbye.

But it is the wife of the Turk that Eoin's eyes follow most eagerly. Even though Eoin senses reciprocal recognition from her husband he ignores it—and propriety—until her eyes finally find him. It is the slowing of the man that alerts his smiling wife to look up and around to deliver the awaited sign.

'Where do they live?' wonders Eoin. How do they manage? How did they learn it all? The woman has the answers, he sees that immediately. The man raises a palm and smiles in a way that makes Eoin hope he might already consider them friends, at least on the road to friendship.

Eoin can see that the Turk is open to friendship. With his wife and son, and all so relaxed together, how could he not be?

The friendliness is not an act to fool the boy in a mode of behavior: he is off gunning and not minding his father by now. It is sincere, and worst of all, it is non-expectant. In his own case, Eoin instantly understands, necessity is missing. In its place is an air of necessity that is simply tiring. It is tiring to maintain but without it there is nothing at all. And just now he understands for the first time that nothing at all is an idea worse than death. Death is therefore preferable.

For all he knows he might love this Turkish family, and they him. They are love-worthy, he can see that by them. He is the problem. He is much harder to gauge. He is ostensibly unlove-worthy. If he were in their place he would have walked quickly past. He wishes they had walked quickly past. They have shown him up to himself.

A faint cold tingling sensation lingers in his lip reminding him of the effect of the dentist's room. How more salutatory it was being there than here, near this family of mystery. Yet the dentist had showed him up too. It was pity he had seen developing through those lenses, Eoin now realizes. It is the same pity, though milder, that he sees in the eyes of this woman who has much less to go on, and only a few seconds to develop it.

'Hello?' comes the distant voice. 'Hello!'

How might the wife and mother feel if she knew the emptiness that this telephone cultivated, widened during the few seconds that she looked into his face, and he back at hers for some truth that he can accept about his life, for instruction on how he should feel; she who knows how to manage living so much better than he; he who is no different from her husband really: they spend the best part of each day the same way. Was that not proof of something deserved?

There is a resounding clack when the Mancunian hangs up. The woman's eyes glance at the hand that holds the handset, registers the shorn knuckle no doubt. But Eoin proves her wrong.

'I'm still here Claire. Just a second.' He nods and smiles to make his eyes smaller, and the couple, grateful for his recognition continue past him slightly quicker, he thinks, than they approached. At the crest of an incline the little boy stands, looking back to see if something is wrong, as if he were the one where all the bucks stop.

THIRTY

The work has stopped. At first I miss the late afternoon bathers, and then trace the other evidence from there. The hammering and clanging and revving have all stopped. At night, from outside, the new building is shaded by the trees I enjoy, by day, from inside. So the final color is to be beige, or grey, as far as I can guess by moonlight from the unshaded parts above the tree tops, comparable with the dirty sand that lies in a pile equal part concrete rubble—I scoop up a handful and examine it—where a stand of palm saplings have been planted.

Some day these new walls and roofs will be torn down, the shallow foundations dug up, and the building work will resume on the same spot. At future sixes—maybe it will be sevens then, or fives—the as yet unborn workers will turn their backs on their labor and the sea will be all they care for. For the remainder of the day.

As it races through my mind I identify the scene of the old man in slippers before it disappears. It is the morning of the first day at school while Eoin's mother is on one knee speaking to the boy, knowing but not telling him that they will never speak again. And so the boy only half-listens because her words are unusual, difficult words, and he does not want to unsettle her with too much attention that could be misconstrued. She is acting, Eoin thinks, for the sake of the mothers and fathers and their children who are passing by. But he merely glances at them because he suspects they can see that his mother is acting and he does not want to allow them to confirm the truth of their reckoning in his eyes. What he focuses on—what his mother pulls his attention away from to say her heroic words—is the old man in slippers across the street.

He is staring with his mouth agape, one shoulder sagging and the other hand at the back of his wispy skull, at a vacant plot of ground that stands between two old buildings. The earth has been excavated to below street level. Shiny teeth-marks from the digger are all around the soil walls of the pit. Of the house that his attitude suggests had stood there when the old man was born, not a trace remains. Nor of the people who once lived in it. Of the people that removed it all there is not a sign either. Was Eoin not seeing, during those moments, an old man putting his old memory under the gun, which is what held his old body fixed in that spot, helpless to move away; the only person with no special place to go that morning, or possibly ever again?

The arrival of the Japanese is the last and definite sign. They bring with them the expectation that they seem to carry to every place they travel: the expectation of failed expectations. I can imagine their reaction. They would not be happy with the result but, as this was Cambodia and not Japan, it would have to do.

The more talking the Cambodians do the worse it will be for them, but who would listen to that coming from me? I hear the voices come and go on the breeze, the ratio of Cambodian to Japanese is exceedingly high. They are explaining things, offerings born of a desire to develop a relationship, to be found acceptable. They are wasting their time, or spending it lavishly: it is a matter of opinion, a matter of age. A matter of time then.

I espy the manager bowing jerkily whenever he gets stuck for words, leading them across the sand, in front of our building, extolling the natural beauty of the site. Somebody had put him in Japan once, and there he had worked to learn the language with a hamper of motivations no two people will ever understand in the same way. Each of his declarations is rendered suspect, deceitful by the silence it earns in place of the approbation it is soliciting. His greatest force of expression, combined with bowing, is no match for the all-powerful silence.

I laugh, and Suzi and Frank stop yammering to observe me. They are oblivious to the four Japanese sweating outside on the sand in silence. Only I see them. It is as if I exist but for brief intervals, and those outside not at all. Apropos of me, only my laughter gets noticed.

Do not ask me to tell you why but I think they come from Tokyo. Who that has grown up in constant fear of earthquakes can find land still enough? Perhaps the wavelets, when they reach the shore, transmit vibrations that to these men, alone, induce a crushing anxiety. Or they can sense the burrowing of innocent crabs that appear skittering, only at night, about which I could tell them something if I could be less sure my words would be incompatible with their expectations.

*   *   *

In his dream on the night of the phone call, and the Turk with his family, Eoin is with his mother again. She is slurping thin white-turnip soup. A strong bleaching sun is coming in the window upon her face and the table, brightening half of the room in yellow and white strips, creating smotey shadows here and there.

From the shaded zone, Eoin rises from his bed and approaches her. Her bowed head is wrapped in a headscarf. As he comes closer what he thinks is lusty eating is really mechanical determination. Each monotonous scoop of the spoon is the same, the slurps equally spaced apart. Although her head is lowered her eyes are raised, peering at something through the window. Beneath the four-legged wooden chair her slippered feet piston back and forth among the slimy debris strewn on the floor. As Eoin comes to her side she looks at him. Her face is larger than he remembers. As she begins to smile she turns her head away and retches the pulp onto the floor. Then she resumes eating, gazing outside, sliding her feet through the sludge.

When he awakens from the dream, cut neatly in half by the frontier of light coming under the door, he sees a white envelope on the floor. All along the corridor showers throw water, like complaints, against the hopefulness of the new day.

The note is written in the same candle-flame ink. A few minutes later, when he looks at the piece of paper for the second time with the muzzle of his pistol supporting the upper flap, he reads as one can guiltlessly read another's mail; another who is incapable of reading.

Eoin remembers the first German that he left in a bad way, but alive. And all the subsequent ones he has encountered since then with teeth like Brophy and teacher's glasses like Gerry.

Not only Germans but Czechs, Croats, Greeks and Ghanaians; they had all stirred him to defend his life and prepare for the worst, for an abrupt attempt at his annihilation. He was growing used to being prepared. He had become his own protector of his former unprotected self that now lived in a different realm, out of reach and safe. Never to know fright again. Anything but fright. Safe. Safe and alone. Safe because alone. That was how his thoughts ran.

They expected him to be afraid in the abstract. The best way. A blinded bull, the pistol his sharp horns. If he did not go back to them he would go Russian, either alone or by taking Germans or other strangers with him if he had to, no matter which, to be misconstrued any which way by others later. That was how their cocky minds went.

But he had not done either. Not yet. Black and white had been separated in their heads for so long. To kill him for merely running away, or worse: to attempt to kill him and fail would be an admission of grey, that they had lost control, were out of their depth. And what good shooting a knee off in Germany where nobody could recognize and defer to the authority the destroyed leg warned of?

Unless he agreed to their punishment and went back with them it would be grey in Germany.

They were trying to make it look like Aaron had delivered the Cologne note as well, by getting him to use Devlin's pen, capital letters, and adding a signature this time. Ha ha! They knew Eoin would appreciate the significance of the signature: the touch of respect, the whiff of compromise. Eoin, they supposed accurately, would not shoot Aaron.

The note had a similar tenor as before but more details this time, more laughable details about Claire: what she had been doing while he was away, where she was now. Then unctuous about the flukes of nature who were gifted, but went off the rails occasionally; that needed a family to thrive, a base to operate from, or else come to nothing. Propaganda from a divine authority. The yellow was an orangey brown where it crossed the blue lines of the paper. The ragged remnants of torn holes along one edge of the page gave the letter an intimate, almost impulsive, quality that went along with the ink coloring. A page pulled from the diary of a girl with a crush.

THERE IS SOMETHING THEY NEED YOU TO HELP THEM WITH . . . was were Eoin stopped and went back to the start of the letter. Maybe they would kill him after all. He thought of negotiating a duel. The quixotic cheek of it would put them in a nice flap. That idea unexpectedly broke open the laughter of the protector inside him. Harsh, rolling peals of mature laughter. All other noises along the corridor ceased as ears pricked for what sparked wonder in even the dullest of minds.

THIRTY ONE

A grenade of fig jam rested precariously on the crown of the mistress's head (a difficult shot), which hid the three-legged flower stand where the jam usually sat alongside one in yellow made from quince whose mysterious disappearance Eoin had become absorbed in. He found himself deliberating which he liked more, the one he could see or the one only remembered.

The fig seemed to have an unfair advantage. It remained for him to judge with his eyes. Or was it to fig's advantage at all? The quince was developing an intangible allure among the gaps in his memory that he suspected was out of proportion to actuality. He could always bring it down to a simple preference for red or yellow, if time ran out. But he would have to decide first, and randomly, then think of a red that he liked better than a particular yellow he liked less. Or a better yellow if it was decided the other way. If he were reckless he would say that the fig was his favorite. It appeared a dull brown in the shade of the lamp but he knew a pile of rubies hid inside, to be revealed when the right light shone through it.

Any spontaneous decision was rife with danger. He would put off deciding as long as possible, turning to the void left by the quince jam to occupy his thoughts.

The mistress described her father's traipse with the fox faint-heartedly. Maybe her father would give up, or maybe she would. With every step, she said, her father saw the importance of his own life dwindle compared with that of the animal (Eoin stifled a yawn perfectly). After a while he had lost the power to be its captor, power he thought he naturally possessed. But he could not take it back now. Perhaps if it were not such a long way to go, if he had not ruined the bicycle, if he did not have to face the inorganic dryness and vastness of the place that was home to the fennec, in this way, on foot. Perhaps, she said, if only he had not had to face this secretly dangerous and ancient land as night passed over it while he, a babe acting old (a babe acting old!), stood before the birth of one whole day.

The desert floor yielded before the light and recorded its superiority. The light that he had forgotten, when it came, aroused the desert inhabitants and recast each thought in his head. He could not remember his ideas of the night before, or of any time before. He said his name: Ulick...Ulick...my name is Ulick. And after a second's delay he recognized something vague. Ulick...Ulick he repeated until it was a half-second, a quarter-second away, until at last he heard the woman's voice as it was coming from his mouth. And he knew why he had forgotten all of his reasons for acting as he did. They had not mattered to him, his mother. They were unimportant. They had all been small and obscure and, now faced with the bigness of time, and the bigness of the world surrounding him, its immense organization, he sensed for the first time how small his reasons were. Even smaller than anything this small fox would do if it were free, because it would still have its instincts.

He stopped walking to better control his bodily activities that had involuntarily begun and to remove the creature that, in the now that was so big, was his only living relation, his only chance for a master.

The sun would appear soon. At first the fox was reluctant to leave the basket. Ulick was a little astonished that it had been sleeping. It shivered, and then made its attempt to escape. He let it go and then grabbed it back an instant later, after noticing something.

Holding the fox up he saw the eye, clearly now, in the early light. It was clouded and when it squinted leaked pus. He would have to hold onto it after all, save the eye or have it removed. Later he would decide whether to release it back to the desert, judge whether it would be capable of surviving. Only now, as he replaced the animal in the basket and discerned the garrison wall in the distance, did he remember he might be shot.

He hurried on his way (probably thinking of the armadillo, as I am right now).

*   *   *

A sulfurous tang leaks from the gun when Eoin takes it apart though no cordite residues remain and the bore shines clean. Nevertheless he cleans it again, with German toilet paper, poking a wad through with two biro barrels end to end as he has done before, following the Karlsruhe Alsatian.

Rust speckles around the breech came off with corn oil, or change color so as to appear invisible. He could not live with a jam. As he rubs and oils, details in his memory clarify through the tarnish of the present. The Browning, in pieces, is a complicated system and satisfyingly familiar. He could dismantle and put it back together under a table while holding a conversation. The bullets feel like puppy dogs, short and blunt-faced, the metal almost soft.

If Aaron were really involved, Eoin thinks, he was not willing. It was inevitable as long as Eoin remained out of reach. Brophy would have inspired his imagination to glimpse something new, using Devlin perhaps, in ways Devlin was incapable of understanding; something that Aaron had not been prepared for. Afterwards Aaron would have forgotten, perhaps without realizing he had forgotten, what he had earlier considered was the right thing to do. He would have succumbed to the plasticity of memory that Eoin now believed he had discovered, of the knowledge that is stored in memories alongside the lie that is stored as words.

By afternoon Eoin is glad to be leaving this kip, to be feeling alive again, to be thinking properly after such a long time confused. He is glad to be getting away from the smell of egg and onion wrapped in plastic, released at the same hour every day. Away from the silent Apaches who only moved their mouths to chomp something reeking and rustling, clutched in their hands, dark eyes dulled to think about the chewing and their fucking families starving back in the homeland. Away from the tireless baby blather of the German Chief, who seemed to need for nothing—not even food—and to whom all activity was play: he could keep it up all day, every day, or give it up and play tennis in the *schwarzwald*. It was all the same to him, or so it seemed in comparison to the Apaches he commanded on the reservation.

Eoin has had enough of it all, is ashamed he has put up with it for so long, that if not for the letter he might have gone on putting up with it for ever more. In this way he is grateful for the letter. It allows him to escape from patterns that have formed and petrified around him. There is no hope for him in this place anymore. There never has been any, a fact he can finally admit to himself. What has held him here is something else, something akin to respite but not exactly that. Something more like cowardice that he is also able to admit. He is more than ready to move on now. His throat rasps from the stale air of his flat that never bothered him before.

To fire another shot would be a relief. At any troubling life, at a coffee-eyed Croat (not even a terrorist) in jeans and baseball cap among a gathering of striped-suited Japanese. An easy shot, taller and broader than the nodding squinters who might have eventually come to like him but would despise him just as much. A vicious animal: no need to eat the likes of him, not even a token piece. Just push the limbs together with the sole of a foot, roll him over with your back turned against any dust raised. The Japanese would reward well and it would be fine.

But to shoot *his own* enemy . . . that would bring a new lease of life.

Listen to me now. The last detail on the letter is important. Claire is probably the reason the letter arrived when it did. They mentioned the baby as a postscript, at the very end, after all the junk they knew he would dismiss.

Below the word CONGRATULATIONS is a grease spot that makes a circle of the paper translucent. He dips a fork handle in the bottle and allows one drop of corn oil to fall beside it and watches as it takes an age to soak in. He compares the two spots carefully. It could have been gun oil. It could have been an accident or it could have been deliberate. But he has found one useful detail in the letter to anchor his mind.

SEE YOU TOMORROW. *Bitte*? Tomorrow? I am ready now! He is ready. And he is not pretending. It might be love, or hate, or the love of his hate that makes his dread of seeing their familiar faces desert him for a desire to show them his. His new face. He is certain it is not fear. He has grown out of that nuisance.

The way in which the French toss a nose in the vague direction of the place they deign to go to indicate what is beneath them resembles Eoin's laugh as he tells himself he will go this day to the laughable address on *Friedrichstrasse* that his devout pursuers have found to hole up in, in his honor, with only coffee or raspberry tea to drink at *frühstück*. People who could not be disheartened for fundamental reasons. The mistress had known that. She had told Eoin they were heartless.

What would she make of him now? But what if . . . what if . . . imagine she were one of them. A ludicrous idea, but how could he be certain she was not? They had women, of course, plenty, foreigners amongst them, Scottish at least: female gallowglasses, waistless demons with a lust for vengeance. Their mien announced their intent. But some looked good. The mistress looked good. She could get away with murder. What if, indeed, after all, she had become one of them? What if she had always been one of them? The thought fascinated him, loosened his tension. Was it not possible that she had been acting in their interests all along? If so then it did not matter whether she was aware of it or not. The result was the same. Since she was acting out her life like everyone else, who knew what was the real her? What part of her was not some deliberate behavior to bring about what she imagined would deliver her coveted happiness?

The warm loaf had never materialized, nor the goat's milk or orange summer kitchen. Yet that was in her, he still felt sure, the real her that he never saw. What he got was cool green and objects preserved in glass, and bath after bath to scorch his balls, and tantalizing fairytales whose endings bored him to tears; to embarrassing tears that she craved so much it did not matter wherefore they came.

How had this thought entered his head? Perhaps it was the only way he could ever be near to her again. The faintest hope had confused his thoughts to land on the improbable.

*   *   *

Depleted, at the end of the desert story, his fingers scattered among the scree were the least of her father's concerns. He used his left hand, with the right raised against gravity, to lift the limp body that he had intended to keep after all, and release after its eye healed. As he was returning it, a round struck and pierced through the basket, convulsing the already dead body. Then no more shots. He should have been relieved.

Through the binoculars of the sentries who had heard the distant shots and spotted the unarmed AWOLer far out on the plain carrying something, his behavior resembled the frenzy of an exhausted man. The shame of it had been awful, he had told her later, she told Eoin. And about the hand that would send him home? Well, it was like a magnifying glass was aiming the desert sunrays upon it. His eyes were busy picking out shadows to give them rest from the building, circling, reflecting sun. Shadows from his body, from the drips that came off it, from the basket, from the torch and the flaccid bladder hooked to his belt. Only shadows rested his eyes.

Everywhere else the pain bore into his brain, and when his eyes were trapped in the brightness he would take a moment to acknowledge it striking, then search for the shadows and respite; moving off again in a strange, inhuman type of way, thinking of something other than the armadillo now.

After the fennec fox's death Eoin lost all interest in the story. His silence had a new basis, at last deliberate. He was doing his part to halt the talking and bring about some conclusion. What she had thought all along, was accurate only for a short spell at the very end.

'Tell her something,' had been in his head earlier. Once it had been: 'Tell her everything.' But not a word friendly enough for his mouth to shape had approached. It was 'say nothing' by the time her father got back to the garrison, and the mistress had become indistinguishable from him.

THIRTY TWO

Outside the *wohnheim*, on the far side of the street, a pug locks its forelegs and leans back on its hindquarters. A woman—a quasi-cripple—drags the dog along. Before each step she speaks aloud to nobody in particular and then throws one of her legs over an imaginary fence, her Christian-red shoes make a stony slap against the ground, and then she turns her attention to the dog once more, to dragging him. Throughout her exertions she wears a look of determined acceptance, as though this business of struggling she finds herself engaged with elevates her, affirms her membership of the town. The club she has faith in is good for her.

She gets the pug into a doorway that might well be her home. Before Eoin has forgotten about her she reappears, with the same unleavened gait. Believing she has become normal, not merely less burdened, by deliverance from the dog, she allows her heavy legs to swing and her feet to paddle the pavement quicker than before. Either she is in a hurry or else she is exulting. She is smiling. Anyone seeing her now for the first time would never imagine what reluctance she had been dragging moments ago, away from the direction she now flounces in.

Eoin wonders if she had the pug with her now, heading in the other direction, would it still resist? Had it resisted on principle? Walking the streets to *Friedrichstrasse* he has the pug and cripple foremost in his mind, allowing guns, bullets, Devlin and Brophy and whoever might be with them, and the *craic* they would all have at the reunion, to orbit at the periphery like jealous whores.

Eoin laughs at 'jealous whores'. It is one of his father's coinages.

On a corner a grand elegant bakery rises up from the ground. On a whim he enters, orders a nice cream cake (don't the Irish love cream cakes and haven't they the teeth to prove it?). A present, a peace offering. A conciliatory gesture. What if everything could be solved with cream cakes? The idea has never become completely ridiculous to Eoin since seeing Bugsy Malone. Maybe he would suggest a pavlova shootout instead of a duel. But maybe they would be in no mood for half-arsed jokes, any sort of jokes, especially if they had already decided to kill him or, being gifted, susceptible and in need of a base, to make him a quasi-cripple they could better frighten thereafter; bring him home in a placid daze. A couple of solid chocks here or there would do it.

It bores Eoin to consider their tired tactics.

The worn oak planks on the bakery floor are imperceptibly cupped. A slight lightening, a greying of the honey-brown grain at the joints offers the clue. Beneath everything in this world, Eoin thinks, there is a resilient grey component. In everything real that we see in nature, in a glass of water, in smoke, dust, air itself seen across certain distances, in skin, hair, teeth, in the sea. There is grey in everything and sometimes, when it shows through, it is more beautiful than any other color around it.

Around the other side of the wall teapot lids, spoons on saucers, floating ice-cubes, Liszt, a smell like warm milk over the mistress's Nescafe granules, and even-tempered voices mingle effortlessly in a harmonious patter. A seemingly infinite capacity for expansion threatens to grow quickly overwhelming. The Browning sulks inside Eoin's coat. It feels cold and foreign.

The thin fabric of his coat is all that preserves the illusion of safety for those around him, he knows. The many undivided notions of safety that are precariously re-assembled every second in this tenth of an acre of minds, like droplets of dew on spider's silk. The unconcern that somebody like him could enter among them.

The *fräulein*, made up with huge dark eyes in flour-dusted clinging black beneath an apron keeps talking in her fluent American. All kinds of questions that a plainer girl would not dare ask. Lying makes her eyes dilate. Every now and then they start, her eyelids going up and coming down a fraction.

'Are you rich?' she says at one point, and while he flounders she lets out a nice laugh, exposing her pierced tongue, and her white teeth, that explain to him like no words could that she is love-worthy. His cock jumps, his balls uncoil from an interminable slumber.

'No. I'm poor. I have to shoot my food. Sometimes dogs.' He taps the Browning through the coat without thinking. She takes a step back from the counter but what does she know about it? In response to her silent reaction he goes on:

'It's lucky I have money on me, or I'd shoot that cake. I'd shoot you.'

'You'd have to deal with my Da.' (What she actually says is: 'You'd have to deal with my Papa.' But what Eoin supposes he hears at the end is 'Da').

'I'd shoot him as well.' His eyes smile, but he controls his mouth.

'That wouldn't be so easy. He's a marine. He'd find you no matter where you went and kill you.' Her eyes bulge, recede. At this point Eoin sees no difference between staying to talk and going on his way—both equally worthwhile, equally problematic, equally drawing. But he cannot do both: one, the other, or neither. Those are his only three options.

When he is outside again with her name and her cake, he feels her gaze following him through the large clean window until he looks back to show her—to show someone—that he is capable of imagining. There has been a flash of surprise, he realizes, the doorway to surprise. A kind of surprise he has known before. Perhaps a superior surprise than before.

'Truth be told,' he begins in his head as he walks along. He had never used 'truth be told', once even swore never to use it. He would consign any utterer, instantly, to idiocy and cheap likeability. But the auld Blarney comes uninvited. Could he have pronounced 'truth be told' on the bakery girl, as easily as he had tapped the Browning, without planning to? Would it have given him the freedom of the idiot, the cheap charmer? What other way was there to go on talking to her without having to screen every word? 'Truth be told' would have been perfect if he could have brought himself to use it. He could have been garrulous. Maybe there was going to be a second chance to use it.

The pug and *crippleen* are ousted, though not completely. They are evicted from the bull's-eye to the inner, Brophy and company shoved out into the magpie, screaming in vain for priority, though it could all change again in an instant. It makes Eoin laugh again. 'Truth be told.' He could use it yet today. Then open fire. On Devlin first. Aim for his diaphragm while his slow engine is warming up. Then take his time on Brophy, leave the options open, discuss life a little, scavenge for the scraps of shame—lean pickings—see if there are any after all. Take a long closing look at his begetter, learn something, teach something or, in the dullest scenario, simply act.

THIRTY THREE

Lives are lived in the autumn. The rest of the year is preparation for autumn. Lives are also lived in the evening and the rest of the day is preparation for evening. I do not want an argument. I am only telling you what I have come to know. You can debate it with somebody else. But ask first if it is autumn or not, evening or not; whether your discussion is preparation for or living itself.

Autumn is spreading her German colors over Karlsruhe, and across the probable world. Night rain hides, during the bluesky day, in the gaps on the ground. Some of it shines on the stretched fallen leaves, on the black tires of bicycles and cars, and in pools on painted windowsills. The shortening of time stirs the autumn heart to action. Soon all will be bare, and all will seem colorless. Even the sky. You are within the climax of the year. You sense too that the anti-climax that you have also been waiting for must happen soon too, or else never. That is what you think.

Eoin walks, trying to place a value on each step. Each toe presses against the sole of its shoe, tearing at it for friction. Each stride is equal and measured, each footstep momentarily patient upon the pavement but light as the half-cripple's had been heavy when called upon to move again. A little rap on the clavicle from the muzzle each time. A physician auscultating a healthy lung to remind himself how a sick one sounds. 'Ninety-nine' Eoin says to set up a nice thoracic vibration for the good doctor. Ninety-nine.

Just then he runs into some difficulty because the Woolworth's ninety-nine had been unironic. Truth be told, splendid. The brittle flake was an effort for the woman to push into the cold hard ice-cream, which in turn was an effort to lick but what came off was a vanilla cream that exceeded all expectations. The stainless steel cages that he could barely see into, with colored sugar-crystals in sparkling piles he promised to explore carefully, later, when there was more time, starting his panic over time. He realized he had to let them go, hope they would wait for another day.

Thinking then about the things that would have to happen (because everything had to have its turn, that is only fair after all) between now and that other day, if it were ever to come again—he could not be sure—became his worry. But the cages of sweets would be something to look forward to, as the other things took their turn to happen, if he could remember them. He would try. If he could believe he, or someone close, would not die before then. If he could make space in his thoughts for a hope that was laughably... no, he probably would not have found that laughable then, just improbable, but no more so than anything else had been. That Woolworth's would naturally follow on from something as awful as that, 'that' being the thing whose turn to happen next after Woolworth's, and making him nostalgic for Woolworth's the very moment he was back outside on Henry Street, and spoiling—at the risk of becoming an ungrateful little prick—his opening pleasure in the ninety-nine, creating a pulse in his stomach (butterflies his mother called it, but later on denied the term existed, let alone that she had even uttered it, when he tried to probe the metaphor while his father was in earshot). Each delicious lick made him feel he might shit his pants.

'Eyes bigger than your belly.' His father's joke. Then taking the ice cream from him, and finishing it off before they reached the Curzon, all except for the dry hollow end of the cone. He threw that in the bin by the glass door as they passed inside before stepping across the red carpet with black zigzags for the wildlife matinee.

The zoologist's narration, the bears, and the sun all seem to go on forever. No start, no middle and no end. The millions of empty seats and odor of stale smoke suggest a holocaust. Slowly, the bears strip the skins off and throw the rest of the salmon away, to float off down the gushing river. Water sparkles on the fur of their bear-chins. The blue sky presses down an ominous, dark shade of pristine. The grass is very green, and long: it would be tiring to walk through, his father would be thinking, he thinks. The Christmas-tree trunks in the background are brown. Sometimes the wet bears look black in the sun but they are all in fact brown because they are grizzlies, his father told him. Like Ben then, but where was old Jack with his noisy mule? Eoin's heart begins to ache for old Jack, and his endless and familiar predicaments. He is surely in one now, somewhere out of sight. Somewhere, Number Seven has a hoof trapped in the rotten planking over a derelict mine shaft. He listens for braying behind the Narrator's drone. There are too many bears about, and the voice's owner never makes a physical appearance. He remains hidden from sight and relentless. No people for Eoin to see at all.

Eoin finally gives up hope of seeing the likes of old Jack and Grizzly Adams, and starts waiting instead for getting back outside on to Abbey Street and to preparing to face whatever would have to come next.

On the way home his father buys him a pair of shoes. They are too small.

'Roughly,' he says to the girl.

'Well I would have to measure his foot now, to know.' She seems unimpressed by his cavalier attitude. But for some reason he does not like to buy the shoes on those terms so he goes again with his 'Roughly what size?' Then, more inflexible than she, he finally cuts her protestations off with another 'Just roughly. Roughly what size?'

To be fair her guess is not far off. No, it is probably bang on, the same size as the shoes Eoin is wearing at the time that are too tight. There is no need to remove them, his father tells him, tapping his shoulder with a finger. The money, stripped off so lavishly, so expressively, from the wad is an unaccountably sad sight. Perhaps it is the tired turn in the girl's manner that is sad, or the time of day, the shop is about to close, already given up hope of further business until Monday, the shutter-pole brought out, when this mockingly urgent sale occurs that echoes back mockery of the buyer and his kin. Maybe it is the thought of his mother that money always inspired, especially watching his father wasting it.

Or perhaps it is simply the sadness of his father, greater for his determination to hide it behind his idea of kindness, which the girl has to go along with because of her job. To abet.

But maybe it is not sad at all. Maybe it is happy. Maybe it is just sad now. So I am not going to swear to it. But if I remember it differently later, I will try to remember to put you straight. If I remember, try to remember. Do you hear that? Ha ha! No, I am happy now. Yes, the sadness was then. I am quite sure of that now. It used to lie in small patches all about the place, wherever vulnerable peace was: in made-up jigsaws, deserted buildings, reflecting water, and sunlight. In female shop assistants, the shops they worked in before closing time, in their obligatory pre-meditated kindness, in shoes, in creamy confectionary.

Eoin releases the twine and the cake hits the ground, making a wet sound that cannot be unmade. The pound of mincemeat that, sneaking up behind him as he walked home, Doran's friendly mongrel bit into, breaking open the rancid-smelling plastic bag the butcher had put it in, made a similar pathetic sound when Eoin tried to kick the dog and it all emptied onto the ground. It had said VICTUALLER outside the butcher's shop. HIGH CLASS VICTUALLER. And just afterwards a kick from a boy to imitate the one with which his father once lifted a

Labrador into the canal, one calm clear morning.

'I am not a child anymore!' He swings his foot at the invisible dog and the box holds its contents until it strikes the trestle frame of a passing pram, splitting at one corner. Eoin fastens his eyes on the wedge of clementine and splash of cream deposited on the ordinary young woman's knee. The Browning, after lurching out of his pocket, hits his jawbone like a reprimand and then returns to its seat, giddy now with self-consciousness.

When she stops and looks at him, fearlessly—not belligerently, just without any fear—it is not because she knows him personally, but because she thinks she knows his kind. Her look says that even your worst act will be tolerated because you are merely a child:

'If you were an adult you would know better. If you were an adult you would not want to hurt another person indiscriminately. If you were an adult I would be afraid of you, but I am showing you that I am not. Because you are not an adult, you are a child.'

It is a look that children sometimes receive, and are defeated by.

'I practically know you,' she seems to be saying with her still eyes; grey, green, blue, he cannot decide what color they are because they are too horrible. They are goaty: wide and goat-staring, and her goat-mouth is wrapped in a tight, neat little grin, a round protruding chin that probably sways gently when she chews.

'Your kind, *eine kinder*, I own one of you. You can see the proof with your own eyes,' she seems to imply with her silent stare. 'There is no need for words. I am a mother. I know children. I know all children. All mothers know all children. You see, it is the mother's instinct. A mother knows.'

Probably full of inhaled baby powder—her brain—and a fascination at the ingenuity in baby clothes designs, at the human treasure their price implies.

'So far so good,' her stare says. 'So far I am right. No mistakes so far. Ever since my life was reset by becoming a mother there have been no mistakes. I can do little *gauche* things at home now. I can drink from the milk carton, wipe the butter off a knife with a thumb and lick it, miss showers some days, go barefoot, drop together and forget for a day my panties and tights in one humid pile, let my face go shiny, leave bones in the fish for my husband to nearly choke on, settle for cheaper, inferior victuals from the HIGH CLASS VICTUALLER, eat mincemeat.'

'That's the last time I'll take you anywhere you little prick,' when her child, in a few years time, asks her about the next trip to Rush.

From there everything slowly going to shit, to shite, to a mad woman's shite. Except, in her head, the mother's instinct. That would seem to blossom. If it had a color it would be pink. If not then the inspiration for the color pink.

Like the dropping of the cake, and the kicking of it, the pistol is in Eoin's hand before he is aware of any decision. That too cannot be undone. Not yet at least. Not while he is still Eoin. Not while he is still Brophy. He has not even seen the baby. For all he knows he or she could be fifteen pounds of explosives. There exist women too who can do that, let me tell you. They can make a convincing face, like this woman, and get away with murder. Only when it is too late would anyone know. But then it would be too late to care, one's focus would have moved on, the damage would have become everything, the awe at the damage everything. Awe before the minds that created it. Awe at life.

'It woke me up to the evil in them,' somebody would way. 'Opened my eyes to what had been going on.'

'What, dear, woke you up to the evil in them? What opened your eyes to what had been going on? Pray what, dear?'

'Awe did. Awe at the destruction. The senseless carnage. Shocking altogether. Now I know why I never liked them. My instincts are rarely wrong,' says the awed person conceding, too late, some piety (apt after carnage).

The woman then, naturally, becomes frightened and tries to walk off. But it is too late.

*   *   *

That last sentence, I hope, completes your story. The story I wrote for you. If it helps you to forgive Eoin, know that I forgive him, if you will believe that.

Now do it. Now, stoop to kiss me, my northern god in the sky. Stoop to the equator to where I have drifted from all harm, to discover indifference in its proper place. Show me your face now at last, your shoulders and head. Then show me your cheeks at work, blowing against the sun. Blow me back to a cooler place. Show me which way it lies, and let me go to there.

Together with you.

THE AUTHOR

George Saitoh is the penname of Gary Quinn. He was born in Dublin. He graduated from the University of York in 1999 with a PhD in molecular biology. He lives in Tokyo where he teaches at Waseda University. His art essays, drama, fiction, and poetry have been published in *Kyoto Journal, Aeqai, Clarion, Word Riot, Santa Ana River Review, Janus Head, Gravel, Orbis, Literary Orphans* and others. His plays have been staged in Tokyo and Dublin.

www.georgesaitoh.com
twitter: @george_saitoh